PARTIES, PAJAMAS, AND LITTLE MYSTERIES

best friends Club, ink™
Stick Together. Friends Forever!™

First published by Parragon in 2009

Parragon
Queen Street House
4 Queen Street
Bath BA1 1HE, UK

For other great BFC INK™ products check out our website at www.bfcink.com

ISBN 978-1-4075-7861-3

Printed in U.S.A.

Please retain information for future reference.

Written by Becky Brookes, Rennie Brown, Sarah Delmege,
Kirsty Neale, and Caroline Plaisted

PARTIES, PAJAMAS, AND LITTLE MYSTERIES

PaRragon

Bath · New York · Singapore · Hong Kong · Cologne · Delhi · Melbourne

CONTENTS:

My diary by Noelle

Tuesday 7:46 pm

I practically had a heart attack when Calista rattled the money box under my nose. I'd just been having a lovely daydream about Ben and then WHAM! RATTLE! RATTLE! There was Calista, giggling and shaking the BFC fund box at me.

"Earth to Noelle! Come in Noelle," she said, rolling her eyes.

"Are you actually writing?" asked my twin, Aliesha, peering suspiciously at my blank notebook. "Because all I can see are Ben's initials and lots of hearts."

So, okay, as secretary of the Best Friends' Club, I was supposed to be taking meeting notes, but I just couldn't concentrate! How was I supposed to keep my mind on BFC funds when I'm going to visit Ben in just four days?

I seriously can't believe it's only been a month since Ben and his family moved to Rockington. It seems like <u>YEARS</u>. I'm not joking! It really does!

It's true what they say about long-distance relationships—they are hard work, but having Ben as my boyfriend makes it totally worth it.

awww. I JUST CAN'T WAIT TO SEE HIM!!!!!

I miss him like crazy. I miss doing all the ordinary stuff, like walking our dogs together and watching DVDs. It's hard not having him around. I seriously don't know what I'd do without the Best Friends' Club to cheer me up!

Kaitlin, Addison, Calista, and Aliesha have been totally wonderful and supportive since Ben moved away. . . like, today, when I forgot to take notes about club funds, Calista said she'd write the minutes for me—even though they're my responsibility.

Ever since we started the BFC, we've all had special roles and duties. I got to be club secretary because I'm super-organized. My twin, Aliesha, is chairperson because she's a great leader (and a bit of a loudmouth!).

Addison is our events organizer because she's full of ideas and Calista is a mathematical genius, so she's just right for the role of treasurer! The last member to join the club was Kaitlin. She's great at design and drawing, so we made her our official designer. Aliesha always says that the BFC brings out everybody's talents, and she's right—our BFC roles are perfect for us!

Hmmm, I wonder if daydreaming about Ben could be classified as a talent? If it is I could be BFC's official daydreamer, too!

Wednesday 7:13 am

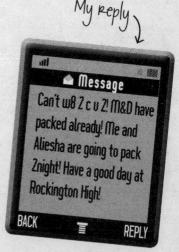

Ooh, a text from Ben!

My reply

Message

Hey, Noelle! Can't w8 2 c u and your family on Saturday! Hv a gr8 day.

xxx

BACK   REPLY

Message

Can't w8 2 c u 2! M&D have packed already! Me and Aliesha are going to pack 2night! Have a good day at Rockington High!

BACK   REPLY

8

Wednesday 5:46 pm

I got told off twice today at school. Once in geography by Ms. McCreadie. . . "You're usually a model student, Noelle, but lately you've had your head in the clouds!"

. . . and once by Ms. Street:

"Did I ask you to doodle the name of your boyfriend? Or did I ask you to do the fraction exercise on page 47?"

Hmm. Teachers so don't get it! Luckily Mom and Dad are a lot more understanding. They are as excited about seeing Ben and his family as I am. Well, almost. I think they're more excited about visiting the historic country mansion that's near Ben's house. . .yawn!

Thursday 7:46 pm

NO!!! NO!!! NOOOOOOOOOOOOOO!!!!!!!!
WHY, OH WHY, OH WHY??????????????

Thursday 8:20 pm

I just DON'T GET IT.

9

Thursday 9:07 pm

It's a total DISASTER.
Ben has canceled the trip this weekend. Everything is ruined. EVERYTHING.

Friday 4:04 pm

Question: Could my life actually get any worse???
Answer: YES.
Question: How?
Answer: Like this . . .
"Hey, Noelle! Did your boyfriend mention that he's in the same class as my cousin at Rockington High?"
I really shouldn't have turned around when I heard Dina's voice, but I kind of couldn't help it. And as soon as she had eye contact with me, there was no stopping her.
Dina the diva is seriously the meanest girl at our school. Her main hobbies are:

A) Being mean.
B) Stirring up trouble.
C) Upsetting members of the BFC.

"Don't give her the opportunity to get to you," Aliesha hissed in my ear. But it was too late. Dina was already dropping her bombshell. . .

"Yeah. My cousin, Sasha, who goes to Rockington High, says that she and Ben have become good friends. Very, um, close, if you know what I mean? Sasha thinks they'll end up dating eventually."

I opened my mouth to say something, but I couldn't seem to speak. Dina smirked at me.

"Obviously, you're going out with him now, Noelle!" she continued. "But how long can a long-distance relationship really last?"

I stared at her open-mouthed.

"Look!" cried Dina. "Sasha texted me a picture of her and Ben together! Don't they make a cute couple?"

It felt like my eyes were being dragged toward Dina's phone. Aliesha and Kait tried to pull me away, but I got a good enough look at Ben and Sasha's smiling faces before the girls hurried me out of the room.

Friday 5:02 pm

This is hideous. I feel awful.

I keep going over everything in my mind. Ben didn't really explain why he was canceling our weekend visit.

What if he can't face seeing me in person, you know, because he's fallen madly in love with Dina's cousin? I trust Ben. I do. Or, at least, I think I do. But what if . . . you know? What if Dina is right? What if all long-distance relationships are doomed to fail? You hear about it all the time.

It's SOOO hard being apart. I just want to see Ben. I just want to know the truth.

Friday 5:20 pm

Aliesha has arranged a BFC sleepover for tonight. I just heard her on the phone to Kaitlin.

"Noelle needs cheering up. Let's have a girls' night in!"

It's sweet of them to try to help, but the only thing that would cheer me up would be to see Ben and hear him deny Dina's hideous rumors.

Friday 10:34 pm

I'm never going to be able to sleep. Never!!!!!!!!!!!!!

BFC Sleepover essentials

1) Sleeping bags, pillows, and PJs.

2) Music

3) DVDs

4) Piles of sleepover snacks—popcorn for the DVDs, smoothies, chips and dips, and as much chocolate as we can get past Mom.

5) Something for Max, so he doesn't try to steal our food.

6) Oh, what is the point? A sleepover isn't going to make anything better. Ben will still be miles away. I will still be here. Nothing will change.

Aliesha and the other BFC girls have come up with a plan.

"Are you sure it's okay to spend the BFC funds on the train fare?" I asked everyone. "The money belongs to all of us. We were saving it for a karaoke machine."

"Listen, Noelle," said Kaitlin. "The only thing that's going to cheer you up right now is going to see Ben."

"Your relationship with Ben is way more important than karaoke!" cried Addison.

"But there's only enough money for two tickets," said Aliesha.

"You should go with her, Aliesha," said Kaitlin. "I'll ask Katie if she'll go with you, too, in case your parents don't like the idea of you riding the train alone. Katie's got a friend near Rockington—she can go with you on the train and visit her friend. She won't mind."

So it's all settled. We're taking the train to Rockington with Kaitlin's big sister. No turning back.

Saturday 5:24 pm

When the train pulled into Rockington, rain was coming down in buckets. We waved goodbye to Katie, who was getting off the train at the next stop.

"Okay," said Aliesha, as the train pulled away, "let's have a look at the map."

"You have the map," I said.

14

"I thought you had it." Aliesha groaned.

"No." I whispered.

We stared down the hill at Rockington. It was a huge town. How were we going to find Ben's without a map?

"Don't worry." said Aliesha, squaring her shoulders. "We know he lives on Rockstone Avenue. We're bound to find it sooner or later!"

It turned out to be later. Two hours later.

I sat down on a wall under the sign saying "Rockstone Avenue" and nervously smoothed my rain-bedraggled hair.

"Don't worry!" said Aliesha, flopping down next to me. "You still look gorgeous!"

My mind skipped back to the picture on Dina's phone.

"Not as gorgeous as Sasha." I whispered.

Suddenly Max began barking and pulling at his leash.

"What's gotten into him?" Aliesha asked.

I pointed at a sign on the old red brick house just across the street.

"It's number 1749! Isn't that Ben's address?" cried Aliesha.

I nodded nervously.

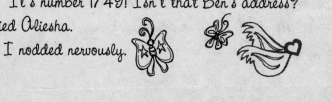

"Let's creep around the back and see if we can see him!" said Aliesha.

"No!" I hissed.

"Come on! Don't turn all shy on me now!" Aliesha said, pulling me off the wall.

We darted behind a bush and Aliesha peered into the front window.

"Don't!" I squeaked.

"How else are you going to find out what's going on? We've got to think like detectives," Aliesha whispered loudly. "Let's check the back of the house."

I followed her up the path, my heart pounding. Suddenly, my foot caught on a flowerpot and I fell forward. I reached out, wildly grabbing on to Aliesha as I fell.

"AAARGH!" yelled Aliesha, as we hurtled toward some neatly placed trash cans. The crash was deafening.

"Oh, no!" I groaned.

"Woof! Woof!" barked Max, thinking it was a game.

"Shh! Max," I pleaded desperately, as the neighbor's dog joined in.

Suddenly, the back door whooshed open and there was Ben's dad. It was one of the most C-R-I-N-G-E-Y moments of my life <u>E-V-E-R.</u>

We looked up at him, brushing bits of garbage out of our hair.

"Hello, girls! he laughed. "Nice of you to drop in!"

Mr. Michelson told us that Ben had canceled our weekend trip so he could pay me a surprise visit!

"Looks like you both had the same idea!" he chuckled.

"Now, how about some hot chocolate? You look frozen!"

Ben's dad went into the kitchen and started clattering around.

"You should call him," Aliesha whispered.

"Who? Ben's dad?" I replied.

"No. Duh. Your boyfriend," giggled Aliesha.

I took my cell phone out of my pocket and stared at it. What was I supposed to say? Oh, hi! I've just been crawling around in your trash cans! Uh, by the way, do you still like me or are you into Dina's cousin?

Suddenly, my phone started ringing. It was Ben! I took a breath and pressed the green button.

The next ten minutes whizzed by in a blur. Ben told me he'd seen the BFC girls, and they'd told him everything.

"I think about you all the time," I whispered.

"Me too," he whispered back. "Hey, how soon can you come home? I'm staying at Jake and Addison's house tonight. Hurry home and we can all hang out!"

So Ben's dad dropped me and Aliesha at the train station and we came home as fast as we could.

In five minutes, my gorgeous, faithful boyfriend will come to our house, just like he used to. And no matter how far apart we live, I know we'll be together forever, just like the BFC!

Ooh, there's the doorbell! Gotta go!

Noelle + Ben
4eva

18

My Diary
by Calista

$$2\sqrt[\heartsuit]{1}$$

$$2 - 1 = \heartsuit$$

Monday 5:05 pm

It may sound weird, but I love Monday mornings. On Mondays, we always have math first period, right after homeroom, and it's totally my favorite subject. Aliesha, who's more into music and drama, hates it.

"You're not normal!" she gripes at me, pretty much every Monday morning.

Today, though, was different. As we were getting settled in homeroom, Ms. Street—she's our homeroom teacher—came in followed by a tall, dark-haired boy.

"Who's he?" said Aliesha, sitting up and looking suddenly loads more awake.

"Good morning," said Ms. Street. "This is Zac Jones. He's new to Green Meadow, so I'd like you all to make him welcome. Zac, there's a spare desk right over there."

Zac walked over to the desk in front of Addison's. Aliesha had this dreamy grin on her face. I didn't get it myself. I mean, Zac was good-looking, but I generally prefer boys who are sort of geek-ishly cute.

Aliesha
loves
Zac

My dream boy

Messy, not-too-trendy hair
I ♡ freckles
Preppy jeans
Funky glasses
Crooked smile
Geek-a-licious tank-tops rock!
Scruffy sneakers

The other thing that put me off is that Zac isn't exactly bright. He also put up his hand in geography and told Ms. McCreadie that the capital of France was Germany.

Germany? **Duh!**

Tuesday 6:25 pm

Not only is Aliesha getting a major crush on Zac, Dina likes him, too. She practically dragged him over to sit with her at lunch.

Thursday 3:55 pm

Today we had the best drama class <u>EVER!</u>

Ms. Harrison put us into pairs and poor Aliesha got stuck with Dina. We were supposed to be acting out a scene from the book we've been reading in class, but Aliesha and Dina were more interested in impressing Zac.

"How could you do this?" said Aliesha in a seriously over-dramatic voice, when it was her turn.

"You know it isn't my fault," said Dina, faking a sob, as she checked out Zac, too.

"If only you knew how it felt to be me," sang Aliesha in reply. "Only your love can set me free," Aliesha went on, gazing over at Zac. He had this kind of stunned expression on his face, although to be honest, so did most of the class.

"You'll never understand how much it means", sang Dina, who was obviously determined not to be out-performed by Aliesha.

"Thank you, girls," interrupted Ms. Harrison. "That was . . . ahem . . . an interesting interpretation of the scene."

"Seriously, Aliesha," said Addison, as we walked out of class a bit later. "What were you thinking?"

"Can I help it if my natural talent overflows once in a while," said Aliesha.

22

"You were totally showing off for Zac Jones," said Kaitlin.

"It's called performing," Aliesha protested.

"OK," said Noelle, "You were totally performing for Zac."

Aliesha grabbed her twin's arm. "D'you think he noticed me?" she said.

"Aliesha," I grinned, "everyone noticed you."

Friday 7:20 pm

I am officially Zac Jones's new study-buddy. Ms. Street kept me behind after school today to ask if I'd help him with some extra math homework.

She said he needs a tutor until he catches up with the rest of the class.

"You're so lucky," said Aliesha. "Think of how much time you'll get to spend with him."

"At least it'll keep him away from Dina," said Addison.

"True," said Aliesha. "And when Calista tells him how amazing I am, he'll realize we're perfect for each other and ask me out."

Ok, I take it back—Zac Jones is actually pretty cool. He came over this morning for our first study session, and he's smarter than I thought.

It was kind of weird, having a boy I hardly know hanging out at my house, especially when we took a snack break, but once we started talking, it turned out we got along really well. Convo between me and Zac:

I asked him:

> What d'you think of Green Meadow so far?

#'s

And Zac went:

> It's cool. Better than my last school.

So I said:

> So have you just moved here?

Zac wrinkled his nose, which was sort of cute:

> No. I used to go to Spring Vale.

24

It's a school not far from here, so I asked:

> How come you left?

Zac admitted:

> I was getting really bad grades. Mom and Dad thought I might do better at a different school.

Lame reply alert:

> Well, Ms. Street's a really good teacher.

Unbelievably, Zac said:

> So are you.

BLUSH-O-RAMA!

Saturday 2:30 pm

I feel awful. I've just realised I didn't mention Aliesha at all when Zac was here. We've got another study session on Tuesday, so I'll have to make up for it then.

Monday 3:45 pm

Zac just caught up with me on the way out of school to say he got a really good grade on the homework we did together.

"You're a legend," he grinned. "See you tomorrow?"

"Sure," I nodded, and as he dashed off, I saw Dina the Diva glaring in my direction.

Tuesday 8:30 pm

Can you believe I just did my homework at this totally cool juice bar in town? Zac persuaded me to go to The Juice Place with him. At first I thought maybe he was trying to get out of doing any homework, but he soon got out his textbooks.

| Invite | Block | Send File | Save | Display Pictures |

To: Calista100

 Aliesha4eva: So, did you talk to Zac about me?

 Calista100: Yup. On the way back from The Juice Place, I told him how amazing you were in Grease last term.

 Aliesha4eva: What?

 Calista100: When you played Sandy in Grease.

 Aliesha4eva: No, the bit about The Juice Place.

 Calista100: Oh, yeah. We went there to study.

 Aliesha4eva: That's a date place, not a studying place.

 Calista100: As if! We were doing homework. And I told him how cool you are.

 Aliesha4eva: Hmmm.

Calista100: IT WAS NOT A DATE!

Send

27

Wednesday 6:55 pm

Aliesha is kind of getting on my nerves. She's been going on and on about me and Zac all morning.

"He's totally had an influence on you," she said.

"How?" I said.

"Well, he's all spontaneous and rebellious," she said, "and you're a bit more . . ."

"Sensible?" suggested Addison.

"Exactly," said Aliesha. "Boring, you mean?" I said.

"No!" the others all said together.

"It's just that he makes you a little more spontaneous," Noelle said, "and you make him more sensible."

"That's all Aliesha meant," said Noelle.

Aliesha sniffed, like it totally wasn't what she'd meant.

But what am I supposed to do? I can't help it if I get along with Zac, or if I spend more time with him than Aliesha. I'm his tutor, that's all. At least, I think it is.

Thursday 12:55 pm

In homeroom this morning, Dina went around the whole class handing out envelopes to everyone except me.

You're invited to my karaoke party!

On: Saturday at 7:30 pm
At: 32 Willow Avenue

R.S.V.P.

Love, Dina

"You have to be kidding," said Addison, opening her envelope and handing me the invitation to read. "How come she's inviting us?"

"To make it more obvious she isn't inviting me," I said.

"She saw me talking to Zac the other day," I explained.

"She's jealous," said Addison.

"No way are we going without you," said Noelle.

I shrugged. "It's fine. I don't care."

"Maybe we should go," said Aliesha. "You know, to find out what Dina's up to."

Invite **Block** **Send File** **Save** **Display Pictures**

To: Calista100, Aliesha4eva, AddisonSportsStar, SmileyNoelle

Kaitlin.New.Girl: Hey C! Good weekend?

AddisonSportStar: We missed you last night at Dina's.

Calista100: So, what happened?

Aliesha4eva: Dina hardly left Zac alone for two seconds.

Kaitlin.New.Girl: It was totally cringey.

AddisonSportStar: She kept trying to make him dance with her.

SmileyNoelle: He soooo isn't in to her.

Kaitlin.New.Girl: We heard her telling him he should get a new homework tutor and saying she was loads brainier than you and more interesting.

SmileyNoelle: Aliesha decided to get revenge, so she accidentally (ha!) spilled juice all over Dina's dress.

Calista100: What did she do?

SmileyNoelle: Walked out and didn't come back.

Calista100: She left her own party?

Aliesha4eva: Yup.

Send

Sunday 7:20 pm

My friends are the best. I mean, sticking up for me like that when I wasn't even there? I should've known Aliesha would never put her crush on Zac before our friendship.

Monday 3:45 pm

Aliesha is unbelievable! I just went to get a book out of my backpack, and found this PHOTO. I don't know where it came from, although I saw Dina hanging around my desk after lunch, and the pic is from her party. So much for Aliesha putting friendship before her crush. She was totally cozied up with Zac! They were sitting really close together, with Aliesha whispering something in his ear, and Zac looking totally happy.

Things this photo makes me feel:

1. Confused – do I just like Zac as a friend, or am I getting a crush on him?
2. Jealous – does that mean it is a crush?
3. Angry – how could Aliesha do that to me?

<u>Tuesday 7:55 pm</u>

I sooo didn't feel like going to school this morning. I didn't want to see Aliesha, Zac, or Dina.

By recess, though, there was nowhere left to hide. The BFC cornered me at one of the picnic tables.

"Ok, spill," said Addison, getting straight to the point.

"You can stop covering up for Aliesha," I said. "I know what really happened at the party."

"What d'you mean?" said Aliesha.

I handed her the photo.

"Where did you get this?" she said.

"Dina."

"We weren't flirting or anything," said Aliesha.

"Yeah, right," I said.

"They weren't!" said Addison. "After Aliesha got rid of Dina, she spent ages telling him how cool you are."

"He asked where you were before we left," added Noelle.

"Really?" I said, and my stomach sort of flipped over.

"Really," nodded Noelle.

"So . . . Do you have a crush on him?" Aliesha asked.

"Shut up!" I giggled, and as Aliesha joined in, I knew the BFC was totally back to normal.

MY DIARY BY ADDISON

Sunday Afternoon

Dina and her crew are VILE!

IT'S OFFICIAL. I CANNOT BELIEVE THE LENGTHS SHE, AND ALL HER DWEEBS, ARE PREPARED TO GO TO TO CAUSE TROUBLE AMONG THE BFC. OBVIOUSLY, THEY DO IT BECAUSE THEY ARE JEALOUS.

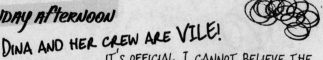

JEALOUS OF -
1. OUR UNBREAKABLE FRIENDSHIPS
2. THE AMOUNT OF FUN WE HAVE TOGETHER
3. OUR FANTASTIC LOOKS
4. OUR AMAZING TALENTS
5. THE FACT THAT WE ARE MORE POPULAR WITH EVERYONE ELSE THAN THEY ARE!

DINA'S BEHAVIOR AT HER PARTY WAS UNBELIEVABLE—EVEN FOR HER! BUT THE BFC HAS PROVED THAT WE ARE BETTER THAN HER AND IT IS SUCH A RELIEF THAT WE'VE SETTLED THE MESS DINA MADE BETWEEN CALISTA AND ALIESHA.

I HAVE ONLY ONE REGRET: THAT I DIDN'T GET A PHOTO OF DINA WITH MY PHONE WHEN SHE WAS STANDING AT HER PARTY DRIPPING WITH ALIESHA'S RATHER WELL-AIMED DRINK!

Monday—after school

I have **BIG** news! Mr. Chester, our principal, made a really important announcement in assembly this morning! It's going to be the district mini-triathlon next month and the school has to select one girl and one boy to represent Green Meadow. There are going to be trials held at school next week. I have **SO** got to be the girl that Mr. Chester chooses!

Monday —late

Invite | Block | Send File | Save | Display Pictures

To: AddisonSportsStar

SmileyNoelle: R u there yet? Hello?

AddisonSportsStar: Sorry—yes I am!

SmileyNoelle: Where have you been?

AddisonSportsStar: Training. If I'm going to represent Green Meadow—and the BFC—at the triathlon then I've got to be the fittest girl at the trials next week.

SmileyNoelle: You are amazing Addison! You really go for it when you want to, don't you?

Kaitlin.New.Girl: Hey—can I join you two?

Aliesha4eva: And me? Way to go, Addison! We're right behind you in your training.

Calista100: Hey—wait for me to catch up!

AddisonSportsStar: That's gr8 to know ur all rooting for me!

Kaitlin.New.Girl: Can we help with planning your training Addy?

AddisonSportsStar: Well—it's really kind of you but I guess as the Events Organizer of the BFC I ought to be able to plan my own training program.

Calista100: Yes—but do you need some help with motivation? You know, we could be there to cheer you on!

Aliesha4eva: And there to check your times and stuff!

AddisonSportsStar: Sounds cool to me! BFs rock!

Send

SO IT'S ALL SETTLED! THE BFs ARE GOING TO TAKE TURNS HELPING ME WARM UP EVERY DAY AND THEN GO THROUGH MY PACES AROUND THE TRACK, ON MY BIKE, AND AT THE POOL. IT'S GOING TO BE HARD WORK BUT I SO WANT TO WIN THIS EVENT! I HAVE TO!!

Tuesday After school

Our PE teacher, Ms. Becker, is helping Mr. Chester with the triathlon trials.

She's putting on some training sessions for us and the first one was today. It was really good. The girls and the boys are training together. I did OK but Sophie, one of Dina's drones, has decided she's going to try taking part.

Sophie is my only really serious competition. Worse, she is pretty good. OK—she is very good. She really is serious competition. I can't bear to think she could beat me and represent the school!

Wednesday—late

I am E-X-H-A-U-S-T-E-D. For the last two days all I seem to have done is run, cycle, and swim. But the BFs are great and have kept me going with drinks, group hugs, and bananas! I just couldn't do this without them! Too wiped out to write any more!

Thursday—After school

I AM FUMING WITH RAGE!

LUCKILY, BEFORE I EXPLODED, KAITLIN PHONED.

"HEY ADDISON! SO YOU'RE BACK FROM TRAINING WITH MS. BECKER?"

I CALMED DOWN ENOUGH TO SAY "NO. I MISSED IT!"

"YOU WHAT?" KAITLIN SAID IN DISBELIEF. "YOU OF ALL PEOPLE MANAGED TO MISS TRAINING? THAT'S SO NOT LIKE YOU!"

"WELL I WOULDN'T HAVE," I SPLUTTERED, "IF KELLY HADN'T BLOWN IT FOR ME!"

"WHAT DO YOU MEAN KELLY? KELLY AS IN DINA'S-DOORMAT-KELLY?"

"THAT'S THE ONE!" I GROANED. "FIRST SHE TOLD ME THAT MR. CHESTER WAS LOOKING FOR ME AND WOULD I WAIT OUTSIDE HIS OFFICE UNTIL HE WAS READY TO COME OUT AND SEE ME. THEN SHE SAID THAT MS. BECKER WAS HOLDING TRAINING AFTER SCHOOL TODAY BECAUSE SHE HAD A MEETING WITH SOMEONE'S PARENT."

"I KNOW ABOUT THE TRAINING AFTER SCHOOL BECAUSE YOU TOLD US," KAITLIN SAID. "BUT WHAT DID MR. CHESTER WANT TO SEE YOU FOR?"

"HE DIDN'T! IT WAS A TRICK!"

"WHAT?"

"KELLY WAS LYING ABOUT MR. CHESTER," I EXPLAINED.

"I SAT AND WAITED FOR AGES OUTSIDE HIS OFFICE AND THEN,

WHEN HE DIDN'T COME, I BEGAN TO REALIZE THAT I'D BEEN TRICKED. THAT'S WHY I MISSED ALL OF LUNCHTIME.

"THEN I WHIZZED OFF AFTER SCHOOL TO GO AND CHANGE FOR TRAINING WITH HER, AND SHE DIDN'T SHOW UP EITHER! IT TURNED OUT THAT TRAINING WAS AT LUNCHTIME—WITH Ms. BECKER AND Mr. CHESTER! SO NOT ONLY DID I MISS THE TRAINING BUT I ALSO MISSED THE CHANCE TO SHOW Mr. CHESTER THAT I'M BETTER THAN SOPHIE!"

"NO WAY!" KAITLIN SAID SYMPATHETICALLY. "SO IT SOUNDS LIKE KELLY SET YOU UP SO THAT YOU'D MISS THE TRAINING AND SOPHIE WOULD HAVE THE CHANCE TO SHOW OFF TO Mr. CHESTER!"

"PLUS IT MAKES ME LOOK AS IF I'M NOT THAT SERIOUS ABOUT THE TRIATHLON ANYWAY!" I WHINED.

"NO WONDER Ms. BECKER GAVE ME FUNNY LOOKS IN PE THIS AFTERNOON. SHE THOUGHT I COULDN'T BOTHER TO GO TO TRAINING!"

"WE HAVE TO DO SOMETHING!" DECLARED KAITLIN.

THIS, I THOUGHT TO MYSELF, MEANS WAR!

Friday—after school

I TRIED TO EXPLAIN TO Ms. BECKER WHAT HAD HAPPENED BUT SHE SAID THAT SHE'D TOLD EVERYONE WHEN THE TRAINING

WAS AND EVERYONE ELSE HAD SHOWN UP ON TIME. WHEN I
TRIED TO SAY SOMETHING ABOUT KELLY SHE JUST GOT REALLY
IMPATIENT AND TOLD ME THAT IT WAS UP TO ME TO TAKE CARE
OF TRAINING AND NOT TO BLAME OTHER PEOPLE! HUH!

WORSE! I WENT TO TRAINING AT LUNCHTIME TODAY AND
MY SNEAKERS—AS IN MY ULTRA NEW SUPER-LUCKY
AERO-DYNAMIC SNEAKERS—HAD DISAPPEARED FROM
MY LOCKER!

I LOOKED FOR THEM EVERYWHERE AND COULDN'T FIND THEM!

BUT I COULDN'T SPEND TOO LONG BECAUSE THEN I WOULD
HAVE BEEN LATE FOR TRAINING AND I THINK MS. BECKER
WOULD HAVE EXPLODED!

THEN, WHEN I DIDN'T HAVE ANY SNEAKERS TO RUN IN, SHE
GAVE ME THIS ABSOLUTELY FIERCE LOOK! LIKE SHE THOUGHT
I WAS MAKING SOME KIND OF JOKE.

BUT THE BFC CAME TO THE RESCUE—AS ALWAYS! ALIESHA
LENT ME HER SNEAKERS BECAUSE SHE'S THE SAME SIZE. IT WAS
GREAT OF HER TO HELP—BUT THE FACT IS THAT I DON'T HAVE
MY SNEAKERS AND STILL CAN'T FIND THEM ANYWHERE.

I REPORTED THEM MISSING TO MS. DAVIES, THE SCHOOL
SECRETARY, WHO TAKES CARE OF THE LOST AND FOUND.
BUT SHE ONLY SAID SHE'D LET ME KNOW IF SOMEONE HANDED
THEM IN.

I TOLD MOM AND SHE HAS GONE **BALLISTIC!**

SHE ONLY BOUGHT THE SNEAKERS FOR ME A FEW WEEKS AGO
AND SAYS I CAN'T HAVE ANOTHER PAIR BECAUSE THEY ARE
TOO EXPENSIVE. I FIGURE I DON'T STAND MUCH OF A CHANCE OF
GETTING A PLACE ON THE TRIATHLON SQUAD NOW. AFTER ALL,
WITH MY TRAINING MESSED UP, MY GOOD SHOES GONE, AND MS.
BECKER AND MR. CHESTER THINKING I'M A WASTE OF SPACE,
I THINK I'VE BLOWN IT.

SUNDAY—really late

EXHAUSTED! SPENT THE WEEKEND TRAINING
FOR THE TRIATHLON WITH THE BFC. THEY ARE
GREAT—BUT MY CHANCES OF GETTING A PLACE
MIGHT BE ZILCH NOW. STILL, I HAVE TO DO MY BEST.
FOR ME—AND FOR THE HONOR OF THE BFC!

MONDAY Night

TOMORROW IS THE TRIAL FOR THE TRIATHLON! I'VE GOT TO
DO IT IN THE AFTERNOON ON THE SCHOOL ATHLETIC FIELD.
I CAN'T SLEEP **I AM SO NERVOUS!**

Tuesday Night

I FEEL SICK! I FEEL MISERABLE! I FEEL HUMILIATED!
TODAY WAS A DISASTER! THIS IS WHAT HAPPENED ...

1. I WENT OFF TO CHANGE FOR THE TRIALS.
2. I COULDN'T OPEN MY LOCKER—MY KEY JUST DIDN'T WORK! NONE OF THE BFs' KEYS WORKED!
3. ALL MY TRIATHLON CLOTHES WERE IN THE LOCKER!
4. NONE OF THE BFC HAD THEIR PE CLOTHES AT SCHOOL BECAUSE IT ISN'T A PE DAY.
5. I TOLD MS. BECKER THAT I HAD TO DO THE TRIALS IN MY REGULAR CLOTHES.
6. MS. BECKER TOLD ME THAT SHE COULDN'T LET ME TAKE PART BECAUSE I OBVIOUSLY DIDN'T HAVE THE RIGHT ATTITUDE AND HADN'T SHOWN ANY COMMITMENT TO REPRESENTING THE SCHOOL OVER THE PAST WEEK!
7. SO I HAD TO MISS OUT ON THE TRIAL.
8. SHOW-OFF SUCK-UP STUCK-UP SOPHIE GOT THE GIRL'S PLACE ON THE SQUAD AND IS REPRESENTING THE SCHOOL AT THE DISTRICT MINI-TRIATHLON CHAMPIONSHIPS.

SmileyNoelle: We HAVE to hold an emergency meeting of the BFC! I've arranged with all the others to meet at our house after school 2moro. B there!

Invite   Block   Send File   Save   Display Pictures

To: AddisonSportsStar,

Send

Wednesday after the BFC meeting

School was HORRIBLE today—really horrible. Dina and her crew made the most of Sophie's success and used every opportunity to make snotty comments to me and the other BFs—but especially me. And Sophie was SO sucking up to Ms. Becker all the time, constantly asking her questions about "When we go to the district triathlon." AAAAAAAARRRGH!

But the BFC is just the best. Noelle called our meeting to order and said that we all had to find out just how my locker had gotten stuck. I explained that

IT SEEMED TO ME TO BE GLUED SHUT. JUST AS IF SOMEONE HAD PUT GLUE IN THE LOCK!

"DINA!" EVERYONE SAID AT THE SAME TIME. AND I AGREED WITH THEM. THIS WHOLE BAD EXPERIENCE JUST HAD TO HAVE SOMETHING TO DO WITH DINA. BUT HOW COULD I EXPLAIN THAT TO MS. BECKER?

"GOT IT!" SAID ALIESHA. "EVERYTHING FOCUSES ON ADDISON'S LOCKER, DOESN'T IT?"

"HER SNEAKERS DISAPPEARED FROM THE LOCKER RIGHT AFTER SHE'D BEEN GIVEN THE TRICK MESSAGE BY KELLY," CALISTA AGREED.

"AND THEN YOUR LOCKER GOT JAMMED UP ON THE DAY OF THE TRIAL," NOELLE STATED.

"THE SAME TRIAL THAT SOPHIE MANAGED TO WIN WITHOUT HAVING TO EVEN BEAT YOU!" KAITLIN POINTED OUT.

"CCTV!" SAID ALIESHA.

"WHAT?" PUZZLED KAITLIN.

"YOU'RE RIGHT, ALIESHA! WE NEED TO ASK THE SCHOOL CUSTODIAN, MR. GOLDSMITH, IF HE CAN CHECK OUT THE CCTV CAMERA IN THE LOCKER ROOM TO SEE WHO WAS HANGING AROUND ADDISON'S LOCKER," SAID NOELLE. "COME ON—LET'S CHECK THE DATES WE NEED AND THEN WE CAN TALK TO MR. GOLDSMITH TOMORROW!"

THURSDAY

MR. GOLDSMITH ROCKS! IN FACT, IF HE WASN'T A MAN, WE MIGHT EVEN MAKE HIM AN HONORARY MEMBER OF THE BFC!

HE SAID HE WAS REALLY SORRY TO HEAR ABOUT MY SNEAKERS, AND MY LOCKER. THEN HE AGREED TO CHECK OUT THE CCTV RECORDING—BUT HE CAN'T DO IT UNTIL TOMORROW. I CAN'T STAND THE SUSPENSE!

FRIDAY

SCORE! PHEW—THERE IS SO MUCH TO TELL.
I'LL START AT THE BEGINNING:

1. MR. GOLDSMITH SAID HE'D FOUND A RECORDING OF DINA AND HER GANG HANGING AROUND MY LOCKER ON THE DAY MY SNEAKERS WENT MISSING.

2. BETTER STILL, HE HAD A GREAT PIC OF DINA VERY CLEARLY HOLDING SOME GLUE IN HER HANDS AND STANDING ULTRA-CLOSE TO MY LOCKER BY HERSELF.

3. NOELLE AND ALIESHA WENT STRAIGHT TO MS. BECKER AND SAID THAT THEY HAD EVIDENCE TO PROVE THAT I HAD BEEN SET UP BY DINA AND SOPHIE.

4. MS. BECKER TOOK US ALL TO MR. CHESTER AND WE HAD TO EXPLAIN.

45

5. MR. CHESTER ASKED MR. GOLDSMITH TO SHOW HIM THE CCTV FOOTAGE.

6. MR. CHESTER TURNED PALE AND THEN RED WITH BLOTCHES AND CALLED DINA AND SOPHIE TO HIS OFFICE.

7. HE THEN CALLED AN EMERGENCY ASSEMBLY.

8. THE WHOLE SCHOOL RECEIVED A LECTURE ABOUT BRINGING CERTAIN SUBSTANCES—IE SUPERGLUE INTO SCHOOL.

9. SOPHIE'S LOCKER WAS THEN SEARCHED AND MS. BECKER FOUND MY SNEAKERS IN THERE!

10. SOPHIE HAS BEEN DISQUALIFIED FROM THE TRIATHLON TEAM!

Monday—after school

SCORE! THE TRIATHLON TRIALS WERE HELD AGAIN TODAY (WITHOUT SOPHIE!) AND I HAVE BEEN SELECTED TO REPRESENT THE SCHOOL AT THE DISTRICT CHAMPIONSHIPS!

Wednesday—two weeks later

TODAY WAS THE DISTRICT MINI-TRIATHLON. I WON THE GIRLS' EVENT AND DAN BROWN PLACED SECOND IN THE BOYS! GREEN MEADOW GOT THE MOST COMBINED POINTS, AND WE CAME AWAY WITH THE SCHOOL TROPHY!

Yay!

My Diary

by Kaitlin

wednesday 5:30 pm

My baby brother, Billy, has just started to talk...well, almost. He hasn't quite managed to say my name yet. I mean, "Ka-in" isn't too far from "Kaitlin."

But what my baby bro lacks in speech, he more than makes up for in crawling ability. Billy's mom, Jen (Dad's wife), turned her back on the little tiger for a millisecond when she was getting some clothes out of his closet this morning. In that time, Billy had crawled out of his crib, onto the landing, and into my room. If I hadn't been in there getting ready for school, who knows what would have happened. One thing's for sure, I wouldn't have been too thrilled to find a gurgling Billy at the bottom of my closet later...

...I saw what he had for breakfast and I know how often he fills his diaper (way too often for my liking). My closet would be a no-go area until all offensive smells (and marks—ew) had disappeared. I would NOT be happy! And this isn't a fluke escape attempt from my

baby bro. No siree. It happens ALL the time. No wonder
Jen looks exhausted.

wednesday 8 pm

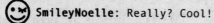

To: SmileyNoelle, Calista100, Aliesha4eva, AddisonSportsStar

Kaitlin.New.Girl: Guess who's hosting a sleepover party on Saturday night? Me!

SmileyNoelle: Really? Cool!

Aliesha4eva: Ooh, I'll bring my fave DVD, "The New Boy," starring the oh-so gorgeous Mickey Dean.

Calista100: Haven't we seen it enough times already, Aliesha? I mean, we even went to the movie premiere and met Mr. Dean himself…

AddisonSportsStar: Correction. Me and Noelle did not go to the premiere (just the after-show party), but we have seen the film a billion times!!!

Kaitlin.New.Girl: One more time can't hurt, I guess. Can everyone come over around 5 pm? Invitations to follow…

Send

Okay, so I'm actually supposed to be babysitting for Billy on Saturday night, but I figured that five pairs of eyes are better than one for keeping my baby bro out of mischief. So, on my advice, Dad is taking Jen out for a well-deserved romantic meal as a break from baby duties. And then it totally came to me…it's the perfect opportunity for a pj party. Jen didn't agree, though.

"I'm not sure it's a good idea to throw a sleepover, Kaitlin," she said, after I told her and Dad my plan.

"It's all right, Jen," Dad said, putting an arm around my shoulder. "Kaitlin will make sure that Billy is her No.1 priority. Right, Kaitlin?"

Absolutely right! I'm going to prove to Jen that I can take care of Billy AND I'm going to throw the best BFC sleepover party ever!

<u>friday 7 pm</u>

Dear Best Friends' Club member

You are cordially invited to the
best EVER BFC sleepover party.

On Saturday beginning at 5 pm. In Kaitlin's
bedroom, at Kaitlin's house. Please bring DVDs,
beauty stuff, pjs, toothbrush, and GOSSIP!!!

R.S.V.P. Kaitlin (BFC Designer)

Everyone LOVED my invitations. Yay! I was up until late
last night making them. Even Dina's evil stares across the
cafeteria couldn't drag me down.

I still can't believe she and Sophie sabotaged Addison's
chances of qualifying for the triathlon, just because Aliesha
(accidentally-on-purpose) ruined Dina's outfit at her party.
Which she SO deserved after flirting with Zac Jones btw.

Speaking of which, I can't wait to get the GOSSIP on the
Calista-Zac sitch at my sleepover!!!

saturday 8:10 pm

NEWS FLASH: Billy is missing!!!

I'm in the bathroom, scribbling in my diary, trying to figure out what to do.

Oh no! Oh no! I'm supposed to be showing Jen I can be responsible and what's the first thing I do? LOSE MY BABY BROTHER!

Okay, keep calm...deep breaths...Billy has to be here SOMEWHERE. Doesn't he???

Everything started off great. The girls got here at 5. Dad and Jen went out to dinner about 6:30. At 7, Billy was sleepy, so I put him to bed in his crib.

"This babysitting thing is a cinch," I told everyone earlier, mid-nacho snack. "All I have to do is check on Billy once in a while. Simple!"

We were all sitting in our pjs on the floor in my bedroom. DVDs were sprawled across the middle of the floor and bowls of sweet and salty snacks were dotted around the room. My bedroom door was ajar, so I could

52

hear Billy if he started crying or calling out.

"You know what?" Noelle added, "Maybe we can add babysitting to our list of credentials in the BFC."

"So, Calista," said Aliesha, suddenly changing the subject. "What's going on with you and Zac Jones?"

Calista flushed bright red.

"Well, if you're not going to answer that, I think we should have a game of Truth or Dare," continued Aliesha. "Let's start with Calista…Truth or Dare?"

Calista went even brighter red and said, "Dare," in a really quiet voice.

"Woo-hooo!" we all shouted, giggling. "That means you love him," Addison said in a sing-song voice.

"Sssh!" said Aliesha, calming everyone down. "Your dare, Ms. Knight, is to walk into Billy's room and remove his fave toy bunny, Mr. Snuggles, without waking him up."

"Oh, you have got to be kidding," sighed Calista. "Not only is that cruel, but it's WAY too hard. Kaitlin, tell her how much Billy LOVES that toy."

"It's true," I agreed. "Billy will scream the house down

when he realizes Mr. Snuggles is missing. Still, while you're there, you could check on him for me…" I ducked as Calista hurled a pillow at my head.

"Pillow fight," Aliesha shouted, and we all started giggling and whacking each other with our pillows.

Mid-fight, Calista must have gone to check on Billy, cos when she got back, she was cuddling Mr. Snuggles.

"You did it!" I gasped, my pillow hovering in the air, a fraction away from Addison's head. Everyone turned to look at Calista.

"Not exactly," Calista said quietly. "Does the dare count if Billy wasn't actually in his crib…or in his room even?"

It took a while for me to register what she was saying.

"What?" I said finally.

"Billy is missing," Calista reiterated.

I dumped my pillow on the bed, raced out of my room and ran next door into Billy's. But Calista was right. Billy wasn't in his crib and I couldn't see him anywhere.

Trying not to panic, Noelle sprang into organized action

and ordered everyone to each search a section of the house. Aliesha checked the living room and the dining room,

Calista checked the kitchen and the downstairs bathroom, Noelle checked the hallway and the stairs, and Addison checked the landing and Billy's room (again).

My area was Jen and Dad's room, and the upstairs bathroom. So here I am, sitting on the toilet seat, trying hard not to FREAK OUT!!! Wait, I've gotta go, someone's knocking on the bathroom door. Maybe they've found Billy...

saturday 8:20 pm

It was Aliesha at the door to say that they'd all finished searching the house and that Billy was nowhere to be seen. Calista suggested that we call the police. Noelle suggested we call my parents. But Jen would kill me. DAD would kill me. I'm not sure which would be worse...

So, I did the only thing I could think of... I locked myself in the bathroom and started to write my will.

kaitlin mccarthy's will

I, Kaitlin McCarthy, hereby request that my belongings be divided up as follows in the event of my (very tragic) death:

1. Sketchbook — for Billy (but only when he grows up. NOT to be used as a scribble book!!!).

2. Fave floaty skirt — Noelle, I KNOW you want it, so it's all yours, hon.

3. Jake Jackson — okay, so he's not EXACTLY mine, but if Gianna Harris is still crushin' on him, I guess she can have him.

4. Pack of five energy-efficient bulbs — Addison, isn't it about time you convinced your family to use these??? Take this pack to get you started.

5. Calista — you're totally welcome to my calculator (it's solar-powered).

6. Diary — Aliesha (but you have to promise NOT to open it until you're older). Maybe you could turn it into a novel?

Uh-oh, did I just hear a key turn in the lock of the front door? That means Dad and Jen are home. Yikes!!!!

sunday 10 am

When Dad and Jen walked into the hallway, Noelle had to coax me out of the bathroom.

"Come on, Kaitlin," she whispered, "they might be able to help us find Billy."

I opened the door and slumped against the frame. "But we've searched EVERYWHERE," I whispered back, before walking slowly down the stairs.

"How was your meal?" I asked Jen, trying to look calm.

"It was lovely, thanks, sweetie," Jen said warmly. "And thanks for watching Billy tonight."

"I'd better go and check on him," said Dad, hanging his coat on the banister and starting up the stairs.

"Actually, about Billy," I continued, licking my dry lips. Dad paused and waited for me to speak. "Um, well, I'm not sure how to tell you this... but he's... " But before I had a chance to say anything else, Noelle interrupted me.

"…here," she smiled, holding him gently in her arms at the top of the stairs, "and asleep."

"Er, of course he's asleep," Jen said, puzzled. "He's normally in his crib by now. Why is he still up? Kaitlin?"

"Oh, well, Kaitlin wanted to keep a close watch on Billy, so he was with us, in Kaitlin's bedroom, the WHOLE time." Aliesha winked at me.

Dad ruffled my hair. "I'm proud of you, sweetheart."

Jen nodded. "It's nice to know we can rely on you."

Noelle had found him fast asleep on a pile of clothes near my closet. He must have escaped out of his crib and crawled through the crack in my door.

"When you said that we'd looked everywhere," Noelle told me, just before we drifted off to sleep, "it reminded me that we hadn't checked your bedroom, so me and Aliesha snuck in while you went downstairs. And there he was…"

And there he was, Billy, the BFC's youngest EVER member—well, as Aliesha said, if you come to one of our sleepovers, you're part of our gang for life.

My Diary
by Aliesha

Tuesday 4 pm

My life is over! Totally O.V.E.R.

I can't believe what happened today! I was at Music Club at lunchtime when Mr. Johnson started talking about the next school production.

"I'm really excited about this one," he smiled. "It's going to be . . ." He gave an American Idol-style pause and I rolled my eyes at Zac impatiently.

"Wait for it," Mr. J grinned, ". . . West Side Story!"

I LOVE West Side Story. It's like totally romantic and really really sad. It was on TV at Christmas and Noelle and I cried our eyes out. Dad had walked in, took one look at our faces, then walked straight back out, muttering "Chick flick" under his breath.

"So . . ." Mr. J was saying, "this year, I'm not going to do open auditions. West Side Story is about making sure we have the best singers in the main parts, so I will be choosing them here and now from the Music Club. So, what I suggest we do is go around the room, and everyone takes a turn singing a verse from 'Somewhere There's A

Place For Us.'"

I wriggled in my seat with excitement. After I'd wowed everyone with my performance as Sandy in the school production of Grease, Mr. J was bound to give me the part of Maria. How could he not?! When it got to my turn, I sang my heart out. Zac winked at me.

"You go girl!" he grinned. "That was fab."

Then it was his turn. The whole room fell quiet, as his clear, strong voice rang out. That boy is totally talented.

When everyone finished, Mr. J stood up.

"That was great," he said. "There's some awesome talent in this room."

Eww! Don't you hate it when teachers try and get down with the kids. So not cool.

"So without further ado," he said, "the part of Tony goes to . . . Zac Jones!"

I shrieked with excitement, as Zac stood up and took a modest bow. I just hoped that Calista would be OK about me and Zac playing love scenes together. I mean I still think Zac's a total hottie and everything, but friends come first. After all, one of the Best Friends' Clubs unwritten rules is: Friends are forever, guys are whatever.

Mr. J held his hands up for silence. "And the part of Maria will be played by . . . Dina!"

What? What is he talking about?

Dina started jumping up and down and screaming.

"As for the other parts, I'll put the cast list up at the end of the day," said Mr. J. "Thanks, everyone. Aliesha, can I have a quick word?"

Dazed, I walked toward him.

"Aliesha," he said, "I just wanted to say that you have an amazing voice, but I can't cast you as the lead in every play. It wouldn't be fair."

"But," I said, "you didn't actually cast me as the lead in the last play. It was only because Noelle was sick that I got the part."

"True," said Mr. J. "But you were so good that I don't think anyone will remember that. Anyway, in this production, I'll only be giving you a small part. Sometimes you have to let other people shine."

Yeah, right. I'm sure that's what big Hollywood casting directors tell top actresses all the time.

I stomped out of the room, just in time to see Dina flicking her hair in Zac's direction and saying, "I can't wait to start working closely

with you."
    This. Could. Not. Be. Happening.
PS: I got the part of one of Tony's second
cousins. I don't even have a name. Great.

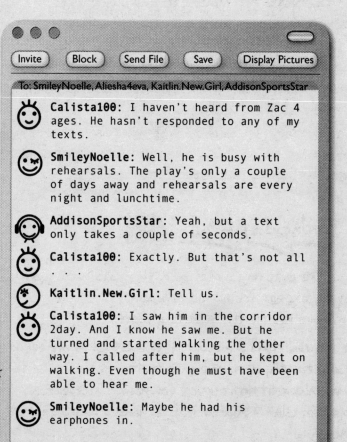

Invite **Block** **Send File** **Save** **Display Pictures**

To: SmileyNoelle, Aliesha4eva, Kaitlin.New.Girl, AddisonSportsStar

Calista100: I haven't heard from Zac 4
ages. He hasn't responded to any of my
texts.

SmileyNoelle: Well, he is busy with
rehearsals. The play's only a couple
of days away and rehearsals are every
night and lunchtime.

AddisonSportsStar: Yeah, but a text
only takes a couple of seconds.

Calista100: Exactly. But that's not all
. . .

Kaitlin.New.Girl: Tell us.

Calista100: I saw him in the corridor
2day. And I know he saw me. But he
turned and started walking the other
way. I called after him, but he kept on
walking. Even though he must have been
able to hear me.

SmileyNoelle: Maybe he had his
earphones in.

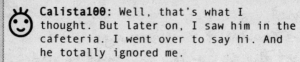

Calista100: Well, that's what I thought. But later on, I saw him in the cafeteria. I went over to say hi. And he totally ignored me.

Aliesha4eva: Nooooooo! What? Totally?

Calista100: Pretty much. As soon as I got there, he said he had to go. And he got up and went over to Dina and sat with her!

Aliesha4eva: Something is totally up. Girls, we need an emergency meeting of the BFC. My house, after school 2moro. Over and out.

Send

Wednesday 6 pm

The meeting's over and the girls have just left (well, except for Noelle obviously!).

This is how the meeting went:

Me: I call this meeting of the BFC to order.
Calista: Oh, just get on with it.
Me: Uh, a little respect for your Chairperson please, Club Treasurer. Everyone listening?
All: Yes.

Me: Good. Right. Well, as we all know something is totally up with Zac. There is no way that someone as nice as Zac would ever be interested in someone like Dina the Diva. Let's face it, she's horrible . . . '

Addison: Nasty.

Kaitlin: Spiteful.

Calista: Witchy.

Noelle: And mean.

Me: Exactly! Something is seriously up! So I have a plan. Your job as fellow members of the BFC is to help me dress up incognito . . .
Addison: In-cog-what-ho?
Me: (sighing) Incognito. You know, in disguise. So no one recognizes me. That way I can spy on Dina the Diva and her posse and find out what's going on. So, any ideas for costumes?
Noelle: Um, a pirate?
Me: Uh, Noelle, don't you think people might notice

a pirate sneaking around school?

Noelle: Oh. Yes. I see what you mean. Doh!

Me: Any other ideas?

Kaitlin: I think simple's the way to go. (She rummaged around in my closet). So if we tie your hair up on your head like so, you wear a hat to cover your hair like this, and a hoodie over that like this. Et voilà. No one will be able to tell it's you.

Me: Genius! Okay ladies, let's all meet tomorrow— same time, same place.

Ooh, I can't wait till tomorrow. Dina the Diva better watch out, that's all I can say.

Thursday 4 pm

You know what? I'd make a terrific spy, even if I do say so myself. At lunchtime I dove into the girls' bathroom and piled my hair on my head and shrugged on my hoodie. Operation Diss the Diva was under way!

I sidled out of the bathroom and bumped slap bang into Mr. J.

"Aliesha!" he said. "I didn't think hoodies were your style."

What? How did he recognize me?

"Uh," I said, "I was, um, cold."

"I see," he nodded, looking at me strangely. Not surprising. It was a boiling hot day outside. "See you later."

I hurtled back into the bathroom. How had he seen through my cunning disguise?

Oh. Note to self. When cunningly disguising yourself don't forget to:

a) put your hat on.

b) and pull your hoodie down over it.

Five minutes later I was back in the corridor, my face properly disguised. Head down, I scuttled down the corridor, my eyes darting from side to side, desperately searching for Dina the Diva.

Suddenly I spotted her and her trusty cronies Sophie, Gianna, Kelly, and Mel next to Ms. Street's open window. Excellent.

67

All I had to do was get to the window without them noticing and eavesdrop. Making sure no one was around, I dove to the floor and caterpillared across the room on my stomach. Can I just say that Ms. Street's floor is in need of some serious cleaning! My clothes were totally covered in dust by the time I got to the window.

Anyway, I pulled myself up into a crouching position and assumed a listening position. Pulling my phone out of my pocket, I dialed Noelle's number:

"Everyone there?" I whispered.

"Yup!" Noelle whispered back.

"OK, put me on speaker. And keep quiet!"

"Understood. Over and out," Noelle giggled.

I held the phone up to the window.

"Like taking candy from a baby!" Dina was saying. "I mean, Zac's very cute, but he's not exactly the sharpest tool in the box."

I felt myself bristle. Zac was totally smart.

"Like what?" Kelly asked.

"Well, like how the BFC has tried to sabotage every single thing our crew has tried to do. You know, like the time they crashed my birthday party with a bunch of 19-year-old guys in tow."

"But that was us!" said Mel.

"I know, idiot!" snapped Dina. "But Zac doesn't know, does he? He wasn't at Green Meadow then. So thanks to me, he now thinks Calista and the rest of her sad little friends are the nastiest girls at school. And he thinks I'm the poor little picked-on victim." She laughed. "It's only a matter of time before he asks me out!"

"What?!" Calista screeched down the phone. Quickly I hit "End Call." But not quickly enough.

"What was that?" said Dina. "Is someone there?"

She turned and stared in the window.

"Who is that?" she hissed.

Pulling the hoodie way down over my face, I hurtled out of the room and ran to the bathroom. Five minutes later, I walked down the corridor, the hoodie and hat hidden safely in my bag. Mission accomplished.

6pm

Well, against my better judgement, the girls have persuaded me not to say anything to Zac about Dina's underhanded antics until after the show. Personally, I wanted to march on stage before the show and announce it to everyone. But as Calista pointed out, that would ruin the night for everyone, and there are a lot of people who have worked hard on the play. But just wait till the after-show party tomorrow. Dina the Diva has really got it coming!

Friday (midnight!!)

The best night ever! Dina made a complete idiot of herself during the play. She came on after the intermission with her skirt tucked into her underpants. When she realized she went redder than a tomato. Hilarious.

But the best part of the night was the after-show party. Me and Calista were in the bathroom when Dina walked in.

"Well, if it isn't the Losers' Club," she smiled nastily.

"Oh, Dina, it's you," I said. "I almost didn't recognize you with your skirt not tucked into your panties."

Calista snorted with laughter.

"Oh, laugh it up," Dina sneered. "But you'll be laughing on the other side of your face when I'm hanging out with Zac later."

"He won't fall for your lies for long," I said.

"Oh yes he will. I've told him all the nasty things I've ever done to you, but said you did them. And even if you tell him otherwise, he won't believe you."

Smiling triumphantly, she turned on her heels. She yanked open the door and stopped dead.

"Zac!" she said, laughing nervously. "What are you doing outside the girls' bathroom?"

"Waiting for you." Zac smiled grimly. "And I'm glad I did. You, Dina, are the most low-down, conniving, evil girl I've ever had the misfortune to meet. I'm going to make sure the whole school knows exactly what you've done."

He looked at me and Calista, "I'm so sorry, girls. I don't know if I can ever make it up to you. But I'd like to try if you'll let me."

Me and Calista looked at each other. "Well, you could start by getting us a soda," I grinned.

My diary
by Noelle

Tuesday 1:30 pm

"So, let's get this straight," said Aliesha, as she bit into her sandwich. "You've got less than four shopping days until Ben's birthday barbecue."

"Yes," I said.

"And you don't have any idea what to buy him?" asked Calista. "Not at all?"

"Everything else is all arranged," I said. "Dad rented a minibus so he can drive us all to the party."

"And we've all decided what we're wearing," said Kaitlin.

"Everything is taken care of, except for his present!" I wailed.

"Even Elliot and Jake have gotten him something," Addison told me. "They bought him a T-shirt. Jake showed it to me yesterday."

"And we got him a book about dogs from the BFC," Calista said.

"Okay, but this isn't really helping," Aliesha said. "We need to hit the mall and we need to do it soon. What's everyone doing tonight?"

Tuesday 8:34 pm

My feet are totally throbbing. We must have walked around every single shop in the whole mall and I STILL haven't found a present for Ben. What am I going to do?

Wednesday 6:25 pm

Number of days until Ben's party: 3

Number of stores
I have looked in: **1 million**

Number of amazing
presents I have for Ben: 0

Despite the whole present situation. I'm beginning to feel excited about the party. A lot excited, actually. I haven't seen Ben for ages. We email all the time and we talk on the phone, but it's not the same as being able to hang out and do all the ordinary stuff, like walking our dogs together and going on dates.

Thursday 6:53 pm

Number of days until Ben's party: **2**

Number of stores I have looked in: **2 million**

Number of amazing presents I have for Ben: **0**

Number of amazing
presents I have for Elliot: **1**

How come it's easier to buy a b-day present for Elliot? His party isn't until the Saturday after Ben's, so it's not even an emergency.

Friday 9:23 pm

I dragged Kaitlin and Aliesha around the mall again tonight. Addison and Calista both had after-school activities, so there were just three of us today. It didn't go well. After about an hour and a half, I'd lost all hope.

"Maybe it would help if we narrowed things down," Kaitlin suggested, as we sat down on a bench. "Let's make a list of ideas."

I found a pen and began scribbling on the back of a math worksheet.

"Aliesha disappeared into a nearby store and came back five minutes later with a can of soda. She opened the can and passed it to Kaitlin, who took a slurp and offered it to me. I shook my head and held up my list.

"Read it to us." Aliesha gurgled through a mouthful of soda.

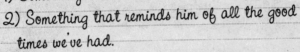

Perfect presents for Ben:

1) Something that he'll love.
2) Something that reminds him of all the good times we've had.
3) Something that he can keep forever (not candy or a T-shirt or anything like that).
4) Something that means something.
5) Something I can buy right now.

"O-k-a-y," said Kaitlin, slowly. "But what about making a list of actual things, you know, like, books or DVDs? Real stuff."

Suddenly, an announcement came over the
loudspeakers.

"The stores will be closing in five minutes. Thank you for shopping at Duke's Mall."

"WHAT???!!!" I screamed. "WHAT???!!!"

"I didn't think they shut for another hour!" cried Aliesha in horror.

Great. Just great. Ben's party is tomorrow and I don't have a present for him.

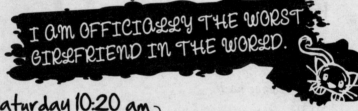

I AM OFFICIALLY THE WORST GIRLFRIEND IN THE WORLD.

Saturday 10:20 am

Writing this on the minibus. Jake, Elliot, and Aliesha are singing Beat Boyz songs at the top of their voices. Kaitlin's braiding Calista's hair, and Addison's talking to my dad.

I've totally missed my present-buying chance now. **AAAAARRGH!** Why didn't I just buy him book or a T-shirt or something?

Saturday 11:50 am ♡

Eeeeeeeeeee! I'm so excited! La! La! Laaaa!

Okay, okay, so Dad just pulled into a rest area, so we could get some drinks and stretch our legs. Oh, this is so cool! Okay, okay, so I went into the little convenience store with Aliesha and the others. And there it was. The Perfect Present For Ben. Seriously!

And okay, to the untrained eye, it was nothing but a mini notebook, but as soon as I saw it I knew exactly what to do.

Five minutes later I was sitting in the coffee shop by myself.

"Aren't you going to sit with us?" called Elliot.

"No, there's something I need to do." I grinned, pulling a pen out of my bag.

I turned to the first page of the blank notebook and began writing a list of all my favorite moments with Ben. The time we both adopted dogs from the Brookbanks Dog Rescue Center, our very first date—stuff like that. Then I started a new page and wrote a list of all the films we'd watched together. Then I wrote a list of all our favorite places to walk the dogs.

Next I wrote down our top ten favorite songs.
I kept writing furiously, page after page of happy
memories and silly sayings we had.

I was just about finished when Kaitlin came over.
"Your dad wants to get going now," Kaitlin said.
"That's cool," I said, closing the book. "I'm ready."

Saturday 9:23 pm

When we got to Ben's, the backyard was full of
people. A group of girls were laughing together and a
couple of boys were flipping through Ben's CD collection.

When Ben saw us he ran down the lawn and jumped
over some flowerbeds.

"Noelle!" he cried, pulling me into a bearlike hug.
"Kaitlin! Aliesha! Addison! Jake, dude, how are you?
Calista! Elliot, great to see you!"

It was so good to have the whole gang together again.
Everyone was grinning like crazy. I put my hand in my
pocket and touched the notebook. I was totally sure that
Ben would love it. I felt so happy I could burst.

Ben called his new friends over and started to

introduce us all.

"This is Lizzie and Harriet and Troy. And here's James and Chris, we play football together. And this is Tara and Megan, and where's Sarah? Oh, there she is!"

We all smiled and said "hi," while Ben told them our names.

Suddenly I felt horribly shy. I slipped my hand into Ben's and gave it a squeeze.

"Now that you're all here, we can give Benny boy his presents!" said Lizzie, somewhat bossily.

"Let's make a pile and he can open them one by one," Sarah cried. I let go of Ben's hand and pushed the little book further into my pocket. I didn't want Ben looking at it in front of all his new friends.

"Don't worry," whispered Kaitlin. "You can give it to him later when you're alone."

But the thing is, we never were. Every time I tried to give Ben his present, Sarah or Lizzie or another one of his new friends appeared on the scene. It was impossible to get him by himself. At first we tried to join in, but they all kept talking about things that happened at their school and other stuff we didn't know about.

After a while, I went and sat under a tree with Ben's dog, and soon the other BFC girls came over.

"That Lizzie girl is a real show-off," Aliesha muttered.

"Harriet is so competitive!" Addison said, sitting down on the grass and patting Sam's head.

"Did you see how clumsy Tara was?" asked Kaitlin. "She dropped her burger in the flowerbed!"

"And Megan thinks she's so smart," Calista said. "She's just been yammering about taking her PSATs early. Like, whatever."

"Well, at least Ben's having a nice time," I said, my voice sounding dangerously wobbly. I looked over at Ben's happy face. He looked so at home with his new friends.

Maybe he didn't need us anymore.

Saturday 9:34 pm

I didn't get to give Ben my present. I didn't get a chance. He practically ignored me all afternoon. He practically ignored us all. Why would he rather be with his new friends? We've known him longer. He belongs to us, not them.

Sunday 8:34 pm

Oh, everything is weird. Jake, Elliot and the BFs are feeling pretty down about the way Ben ignored us yesterday, and I'm feeling totally depressed too.

I wish everything was back how it used to be. I didn't realize Ben would change so much when he moved away. He doesn't seem to have any time for me or the gang.

I wonder if Ben'll be able to drag himself away from Rockington to come to Elliot's party next week? If he's not too busy with his new friends, that is.

Wednesday 6:45 pm

I've put Ben's little book under my bed. I know I'll never give it to him now, but I can't bear to throw it away.

Thursday 8:32 pm

Just got a text from Ben.
What am I supposed to say
to that?

Hi Noelle! Haven't heard
from u since Saturday.
R u OK?

BACK ☰ REPLY

Friday 5:12 pm

Elliot's party is tomorrow.
I feel so weird. Half of me wants to see Ben, but
half of me is angry about last week. Why is life so
complicated?

Saturday 10:20 pm

By the time we got to Elliot's house, I had a serious
amount of butterflies in my stomach. If it wasn't for the
BFC girls, I probably would have gone home.

My heart jumped, when I saw Ben. "Hi," Ben said.
"Hi," I said back.

"Listen, Noelle, come over here for a sec. I need to
talk to you."

He took my hand and led me into the kitchen.

"It's been a while since we've been alone," he whispered quietly.

"Well, that's not my fault!" I cried.

"Oh, Noelle. I'm sorry about last week. I felt so torn between you and the gang and all my new buddies. I know I treated you all badly. I'm so, so sorry."

He explained how hard it was moving to a new town.

"I missed you and everyone so much, and then, as I met new people, things got easier. It sounds silly, but I made friends with people who reminded me of the BFC— somehow it made me feel more at home."

Suddenly it started to make sense.

"Lizzie is just as bossy as Aliesha," I said. "Aliesha didn't like it one bit!"

"But I'm so sure they'd get along if they gave each other a chance," said Ben.

"Harriet's competitive, like Addison," I giggled.

"And Megan reminds me of Calista!" Ben grinned.

"And what did Kaitlin think of Tara? Those two are practically twins!"

"And who reminds you of me?" I cried. "Sarah?"

Ben put his arm around my shoulder.

85

"There is nobody like you, Noelle," he said. "You're one in a million."

After that, we went back into Elliot's living room. Ben went around the whole crew and apologized individually.

After the party, Ben walked me and Aliesha back home, just like he used to. When we got to the door, I dashed upstairs and took the little book of memories from under my bed.

"I forgot to give you your birthday present," I said, as I ran back downstairs.

Ben opened the book and started reading.

"Our best moments, our favorite films, our top dog walks, our favorite songs—Noelle, this is so perfect. I love it!"

I looked up into his smiling eyes and somehow I knew that everything would be okay.

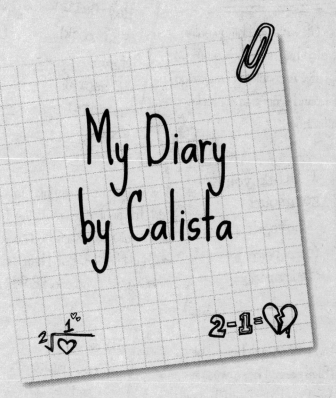

My Diary
by Calista

Friday 4:50 pm

Ok, so something really weird has been going on lately. A couple of days ago, I found a note in my locker at school.

Hey Calista,
You rock!
Love,
A secret
admirer
xxx

I think you're gorgeous!
Love,
Your secret
admirer xxx

It was just before this big math test I'd spent ages studying for, and I was too distracted to pay much attention. But then, this morning, I found another one.

And when I got home this afternoon, there was one on the front doormat. I've put them in my bag to see what the others make of them at our BFC meeting tomorrow.

Hi Cutie,
You make me smile! :)
Secret admirer
xxx

Saturday 5:10 pm

Our meeting this afternoon was at Kaitlin's house, and when I got there, she handed me a note. It was on pale pink paper, just like the others.

> Have a cool weekend.
> Love,
> Guess who?
> xxxx

"Is this a joke?" I said.

"How d'you mean?" asked Kaitlin.

All five of us were sitting in her bedroom, eating some strawberries she'd found in the fridge.

"All these notes," I said.

"All what notes?" said Kaitlin. "Someone stuffed that through our mail slot this morning, but there haven't been any others."

I pulled the notes out of my bag and spread them out on Kaitlin's bed, along with the one I'd just opened.

"I've been getting them all week," I said. "Two at school, one at home, then that one just now."

"Who are they from?" asked Noelle.

"Duh!" said Aliesha. "A secret admirer. As in, it's a secret." Noelle stuck her tongue out.

"Don't you have any idea who it could be?" Addison asked.

I shook my head.

"OK," said Noelle, pulling out her BFC secretary's notebook. "I think we should add a new item to the agenda.

Calista's Secret Admirer

Questions:
1. What can we deduce from the notes?
2. Do we know anyone who likes Calista?

Actions:
1. Make a list of suspects.
2. Investigate suspects.

"OK, question one," said Noelle. "What can we tell from the notes?"

"They're from someone who knows Calista pretty well," said Addison.

"Why?" asked Aliesha.

"It could be a mysterious stranger," said Kaitlin.

"How would a stranger know where Calista lives?" said Addison.

Kaitlin frowned. "Oh, yeah."

"They must've known she was coming here for the meeting, too," said Noelle.

"It's probably someone from school, then," I said. "Most likely in our class."

"Aha!" said Aliesha. "Zac Jones! He's in our class and we know he likes you."

"No, we don't," I said, blushing. "It's probably just someone doing it as a joke anyway."

"But how are we going to find out?" said Noelle.

Aliesha tapped the side of her nose. "Leave it to me," she said. "Aliesha Roberts, Undercover Agent."

I looked around at the others. The idea of someone as loud as Aliesha doing anything undercover seemed pretty impossible. None of us said anything.

"Cool," grinned Aliesha. "That's that, then."

Invite Block Send File Save Display Pictures

To: AddisonSportsStar, Kaitlin.New.Girl, Calista100, SmileyNoelle

Aliesha4eva: Aliesha Roberts, Undercover Agent, reporting for duty.

AddisonSportsStar: So, let's have it, Agent Roberts.

Kaitlin.New.Girl: What have you found out?

Aliesha4eva: I've talked to all the boys in our class, and I still say it's Zac Jones who's been sending the notes.

Calista100: Why?

Aliesha4eva: Four of the boys said they liked Dina, two of them had crushes on Ms. Street, three asked me out, one thought I was Noelle and wanted to know if I'd dumped Ben yet, and the last two had no idea which one of us was Calista. Which just leaves Zac.

AddisonSportsStar: It does make sense. We all know you get along really well with him.

SmileyNoelle: It's a classic case of opposites attract.

Kaitlin.New.Girl: Aw, sweet!

Calista100: But if it's him, why doesn't he just tell me instead of sending notes?

AddisonSportsStar: Boys are weird.

SmileyNoelle: Let's wait and see if you get any more notes.

Aliesha4eva: If we're lucky, we might catch Zac in the act.

Send

I logged off, then lay back on my bed, thinking. I really like Zac, and it was seriously exciting to think he might have sent the notes. But what if I said something to him and it turned out he hadn't? The truth is, I'm way too shy to admit to Zac that I like him and unless he says something first, nothing's ever going to happen.

Thursday 3:40 pm

Yay! Aliesha's invited all of us to a sleepover at her place on Saturday. I thought it was going to be a boring night watching crummy TV with my family, but instead—cool music, makeovers, pizza, and girly gossip. Seriously awesome! It is kind of strange that Aliesha's the one who's planned it. Usually, Noelle and Addison do that kind of stuff, and Aliesha just shows up with a pile of make-up and CDs, but who cares? BFC + snacks + somewhere to hang out for as long as we like = guaranteed fun.

Friday 9:00 pm

Good stuff about today: We found out Dina will be out of school all next week because she's doing an exchange with her French pen pal.

Bad stuff about today: Ms. Street says Zac's grades are good enough for me to stop tutoring him. No more study-buddy sessions. :-(

Weird stuff about today: I got another note.

Hey, gorgeous
girl.
You + me = ♥♥
Love,
Secret Admirer
xxx

Sunday 11:40 am

The sleepover last night was cool. We made up a bunch of new dance routines, Noelle and Kaitlin tried to straighten my hair (sooo not happening!), and Addison brought these totally yummy brownies.

Eventually, we went to bed just after midnight, when Noelle and Aliesha's mom promised she'd make us blueberry pancakes for breakfast as long as we shut up and went to sleep.

We got up pretty early, considering all the hard gossipy work we'd done the night before, and we were halfway through wolfing down the pancakes when the doorbell rang.

"Nngggggg," said Noelle, with her mouth full.

"I'm not finished yet," answered Aliesha, who'd obviously understood her perfectly. "Will you answer it, Calista?"

"I'm not finished, either," I said.

"Pleeeeeeease," said Aliesha. "You're nearest."

"By, like, three inches," I grumbled, grabbing the last bit of my pancake as I stood up.

I walked along the Roberts' hall in my rabbit slippers, munching my pancake, and opened the front door.

"Zac!" I said, spraying bits of blueberry everywhere.

What was he doing knocking on Noelle and Aliesha's door at this time on Sunday morning? I tried seriously hard not to blush, and then, just when you thought it couldn't be any worse, remembered three things.

1. I was wearing my oldest, cringiest, covered-in-babyish-panda pajamas
2. They were accessorized with the bunny slippers.
3. After the whole hair-straightening disaster, I had the worst case of bed-head in the entire history of both heads and beds.

"Hi," grinned Zac. "So it's you."

"Uh, yeah," I said, wondering if I looked that different from normal in my PJs.

"I wasn't sure who lived here," he said.

"It's Aliesha and Noelle's house," I said, confused. "We had a sleepover last night."

"Oh," said Zac. "Well, I'm really glad it's you, anyway." He smiled again. "Mystery solved."

"What mystery?" I said.

"The note," Zac explained. "Come to 12 Grenville Road

on Sunday morning if you want to know who your mystery admirer is".

A whole bunch of stuff clicked into place in my head. Someone had sent Zac a note, just like the ones I'd been getting. I thought he'd been sending them to me, and he seemed to think I'd sent this one to him. But I totally hadn't, and if it wasn't me, who else could it be?

"Are you ok?" yelled Noelle from the kitchen.

And that's when I realized.

"Come to 12 Grenville Road." Aliesha and Noelle's house. Aliesha must have sent the note!

"Aliesha, someone's here to see you," I shouted, and without saying another word to Zac, I stormed back inside and up to Noelle's bedroom.

I got dressed quickly and sent a text message to my dad.

If Aliesha still had a crush on Zac, why couldn't she just have said so? Furious, I grabbed my bag and stomped downstairs.

"Calista!" said Aliesha, who was standing on the doorstep with Zac. "What's—"

But before she could say another word, I pushed past her and went to wait for Dad at the corner.

Honestly, this weekend has been totally bonkers. Kaitlin, Noelle, Aliesha and Addison have just left, after Mom let them in and I was forced to listen to what they had to say.

"I'm not interested," I snapped, as soon as Aliesha opened her mouth. "You totally set me up to think Zac liked me, when it's obvious you're the one who wants to go out with him."

"I didn't!" said Aliesha. "I mean, I don't."

Kaitlin stepped in front of Aliesha and tried to sound calm. "Will you just listen to us?" she said.

I scowled, then nodded, even though I totally wasn't in the mood for any of Aliesha's excuses.

"OK," said Noelle. "First of all, you're right. It was Aliesha who sent the note to Zac—"

"I knew—"

"Shut up!" said Kaitlin, Addison, and Noelle together.

"She did send the note," Noelle repeated, "but she was trying to make Zac think it was from you."

"She knew you liked each other, and she wanted to help," explained Addison.

"We think you'd make a really cute couple," said Kaitlin. "All of us, including Aliesha."

I looked at Aliesha, and she nodded.

I was still kind of annoyed she'd decided to poke her nose in between me and Zac, but I knew she'd only done it because she cares about me.

"I'm sorry," I said. She hugged me, then there was an awkward kind of silence.

"Hey!" said Addison, "We forgot to tell you the other thing."

"Oh, yeah," said Aliesha. "About the notes you've been getting."

"After you left, I started talking to Zac," said Aliesha, "and it's not him who's been sending them after all."

"Oh," I said, disappointed.

"We thought it was still a mystery," said Addison, "but then Zac remembered seeing Dina pushing a piece of paper into your locker."

"A pink piece of paper," said Noelle.

"But I haven't gotten any notes from Dina," I said.

"Exactly," nodded Aliesha. "Which can only mean . . . "

"She's the one who sent the notes," I said. "But why?"

"Duh!" said Aliesha. "To make you think Zac liked you, so you'd embarrass yourself by asking him out."

"Except she had no idea he really does like you, and would probably have said yes if you'd asked him out," said Noelle.

99

And even though I was happy me and Aliesha were friends again, I couldn't help feeling the tiniest bit disappointed that Zac hadn't sent the note.

Tuesday 1:15 pm

I don't believe this! I've just found another note in my locker.

> Hi! Do you want to go out sometime?
> Love,
> Secret admirer
> xxxxx

"Look at this," I said, slapping it down on my desk at the beginning of afternoon classes. "Seriously, why can't Dina just give it up?"

"Uh, Calista?" said Addison, reading the note. "Dina isn't here this week. She's in France."

I suddenly realized the note was handwritten instead of printed.

"Isn't that—"

"Zac's handwriting," I said, feeling kind of dizzy. I recognized it from all the time we'd spent doing homework together.

Aliesha raised her eyebrows. "I told you he liked you," she beamed, and for once, I couldn't have been more glad she was right.

MY DIARY
BY
ADDISON

Saturday morning

Phew! With all the drama with Calista this week I haven't had a minute to write in my diary. All that fuss! Over a boy! Still, I'm glad because Calista's glad.

OK, so here's what I've been up to lately:

1. Hanging out with the BFC to set up the Calista-Zac love-fest.
2. Training session at the pool.
3. Volleyball game at school—we WON!
4. Basketball training last night at recreation center.

Oops—gotta go!

Dad's yelling at me to hurry up because he promised to take me and Jake to the skate park. Elliot's coming too.

Saturday afternoon

What a great morning! The skate park was wicked. They finished a new section and the layout really flows well.

Elliot was helping me out while Jake was trying to master a railstand. Elliot said I was doing really well.

HE'S AN AWESOME SKATER HIMSELF.

HE CAME BACK TO OUR HOUSE AFTER THE PARK. HE'D BROUGHT OVER SOME BRITISH SKATING MAGS THAT HIS UNCLE BROUGHT HIM. THEY ARE SO AMAZING—SOME OF THE PHOTOS WERE JUST INCREDIBLE. ELLIOT EVEN GAVE ME A POSTER FROM ONE OF THE MAGS TO PUT UP IN MY ROOM.

Sunday late

WENT SWIMMING WITH THE BFC THIS MORNING. WE HAD SO MUCH FUN, BUT THEN IT GOT IRRITATING BECAUSE ALL THE OTHERS WANTED TO DO WAS FOOL AROUND. I WANTED TO DO SOME LENGTHS!

"CHILL OUT, ADDISON!" ALIESHA SAID.

"YEAH—IT'S NOT ALWAYS A RACE," KAITLIN AGREED WITH HER.

SO FINALLY I GAVE UP TRYING TO FIND SOMEONE TO SWIM AGAINST AND WE ALL WENT ON THE WATERSLIDE.

THEN WE CHILLED AT CALISTA'S (ZAC KEPT SENDING HER TEXTS!) FOR THE AFTERNOON. NOW I'VE BEEN WATCHING A SKATING DVD THAT ELLIOT LENT JAKE. IT'S AWESOME AND HAS GIVEN ME SOME IDEAS FOR THINGS TO TRY NEXT WEEK.

To: AddisonSportsStar

Calista100: Did you get the answer to question 24 in the math homework?

AddisonSportsStar: What? Homework? Dee-saster - I forgot to do it!

Calista100: Ms. Street will go nuts, Addison! That's the second time this week you haven't done it.

AddisonSportsStar: Well a girl has to live, doesn't she? I barely have time to breathe these days, there's so much to do.

Calista100: But Ms. Street doesn't care about all your sports, Addison!

AddisonSportsStar: No problem. I'll think up something to tell her. I can do it at lunchtime if the BFCs can help me...

Send

Monday after school

Ms. Street is **SO** not fair! She gave me so much hassle about my math.

104

There was no time to do it at lunchtime because Dina and her cronies were hanging around. There's no way I'm letting them see me scrambling around trying to get my homework done. So when Ms. Street asked me why I had nothing to hand in I just played it cool and told her I'd been in a skate competition all weekend. OK, so I told a great big fib.

Noelle nearly gave the game away because when I said it, she pulled a face. I saw Ms. Street glance at her and then look back at me. In the end Ms. Street said "Addison, your sports activities shouldn't interfere with your schoolwork. Even if you have been competing for the school, I expect you to complete all your projects. I need to see your math assignment on my desk first thing tomorrow!"

Sob, sob! So now I'm doing a boring old math project.

Monday some time later

Math is soooooo boring! And soooooooooooo hard! I didn't understand half of the questions, but I've done my best. Who ever needed to be good at math to win a race?

105

Monday bedtime

I thought Elliot was coming over this evening to go through some DVDs with Jake. Turns out he's coming tomorrow instead after soccer practice.

I've been thinking about Ms. Street and the way she went off on one today. Sports really should be a good enough reason for not getting homework done. I mean, fitness is important, right?

Tuesday after school

I don't know why I bothered doing my math homework. Ms. Street made me sit there while she marked it, and then told me she thought it would be better if she put me into remedial classes! Can you believe that?! She said I OBVIOUSLY spent more time doing sports than on schoolwork and I needed serious help!!!

Can she really do that?

Wednesday pm

Apparently she can! I'm now in totally different classes from my BFs!! It's horrible. Dina and her cronies have been crowing about how I've been kicked out because

I'm soooooo stupid. Then the rest of the BFC came to "talk" to me at lunchtime. Here's what happened...

1| The BFC had an emergency meeting **WITHOUT ME** after school yesterday. They said it wasn't an official meeting, they were "just worried about me."

2| They said that Ms. Street had a point (traitors!). They agreed that I DID spend a lot of time skateboarding and swimming and maybe I could spend a little more time studying.

3| They said they wanted to help me.

Oh really?! If they really want to help me, maybe they could just leave me alone!

Wednesday before bed

Elliot is really funny, he made me laugh so much with his jokes that I (almost) forgot about being put in remedial classes and the BFs being mean.

Thursday

Noelle came up to me at recess and said, "Hey Addison. Listen I hate it when you won't talk to us. We just want to help you, you know."

"So why is everyone so down on me?" I asked.

Noelle put her arm around me. "We're not down on you Addison! It's just that we're worried and we REALLY miss having you in the same classes as us."

"I know, but what can I do about it? I'm just not as smart as you guys. So what's the point of spending too much time on homework and stuff?" I shrugged.

"Well, for starters you are perfectly smart, Addison!" Noelle exclaimed. "Honestly Addison, I can't believe that you, of all people, don't care about other people doing better than you. Since when did you ever want to be last at anything?"

It's true, I really don't like being last—especially with Dina making fun of me.

"But homework is so boring—and so hard!" I whined.

"All you need to do is spend a little more time on it, Addison," Noelle said gently. "We've helped you with your grades before, haven't we? Please let us help you do it again! I bet we can get you back in your regular classes in no time if we all work together!"

I looked at her. Maybe they could. The BFC had helped me before when I needed to get my grades up to stay on the school swim team.

With the BFs helping me, schoolwork had been much more fun. Maybe Noelle had a point after all.

"So," Noelle smiled at me. "Will you let us help you? Please? Pretty please?"

She put on a ridiculous grin and looked at me. I couldn't help laughing.

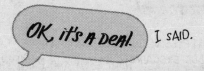 **OK, it's a deal.** I said.

Thursday—later

Aliesha's drawn up a plan of action—a kind of roster of who's going to pair up with me to do homework every day after school. It's cool. BFC rocks!

BFC ACTION PLAN TO MAKE ADDISON'S GRADES TOTALLY TERRIFIC!

MONDAY: NOELLE

TUESDAY: KAITLIN

WEDNESDAY: CALISTA

THURSDAY: ALIESHA

FRIDAY: ALL THE BFC!

Friday after school

OK, SO I HATE BEING IN DIFFERENT CLASSES FROM MY BFs, BUT MS. FRASER, MY NEW HOMEROOM AND ENGLISH TEACHER, ISN'T BAD. SHE'S JUST GIVEN ME THE BEST PROJECT EVER! AND I CERTAINLY NEVER THOUGHT I WAS GOING TO BE SAYING THAT LAST WEEK! I'VE GOT TO DO A PROJECT ON MY FAVE HOBBY. NOW THAT WAS A DIFFICULT ONE—WHICH SPORT TO CHOOSE?

I FINALLY DECIDED TO GO FOR SKATEBOARDING! IT'S DUE IN A WEEK.

THE BFC CAME OVER BEFORE BASKETBALL TRAINING JUST LIKE THEY PROMISED TO HELP ME WITH MY HOMEWORK. WHEN I

TOLD THEM ABOUT MY PROJECT THEY WERE REALLY PLEASED.

NOELLE WAS GRINNING. "THIS IS A REALLY GOOD CHANCE TO IMPRESS YOUR NEW TEACHER."

"YEAH," AGREED CALISTA. "IF YOU DO WELL ON THIS AND GET YOUR OTHER GRADES HIGHER, MS. FRASER MIGHT RECOMMEND SENDING YOU BACK TO REGULAR CLASSES."

I JUST KNOW I'M GOING TO DO THIS BRILLIANTLY AND I'LL BE BACK WITH MY BFs BEFORE LONG.

I DIDN'T KNOW HOW TO START MY PROJECT AND ALIESHA SUGGESTED THAT I THOUGHT UP SOME SECTIONS—THINGS LIKE HOW SKATEBOARDING STARTED, WHAT YOU WEAR, A GLOSSARY OF TERMS—THAT SORT OF THING. COOL! I GOT SOME MAGS OUT AND STARTED CUTTING OUT PICTURES AND THINGS. I'VE GOT LOADS OF IDEAS ALREADY!

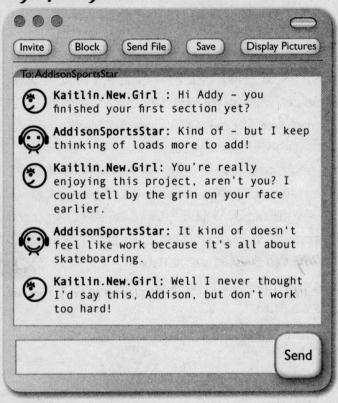

○ ○ ○   ⊂⊃

(Invite) (Block) (Send File) (Save) (Display Pictures)

To: AddisonSportsStar

Kaitlin.New.Girl : Hi Addy - you finished your first section yet?

AddisonSportsStar: Kind of - but I keep thinking of loads more to add!

Kaitlin.New.Girl: You're really enjoying this project, aren't you? I could tell by the grin on your face earlier.

AddisonSportsStar: It kind of doesn't feel like work because it's all about skateboarding.

Kaitlin.New.Girl: Well I never thought I'd say this, Addison, but don't work too hard!

[   ] Send

Saturday—afternoon

I WENT SKATEBOARDING WITH JAKE AND ELLIOT THIS MORNING. I TOLD ELLIOT ALL ABOUT MY PROJECT AND HE SAID HE'D LOVE TO SEE IT WHEN IT WAS FINISHED. HE GAVE ME SOME

MORE OF HIS MAGS SO THAT I COULD USE SOME OF THE PHOTOS.
HE IS SO COOL!

Saturday much later

I AM SO GETTING INTO THIS PROJECT. I'VE DONE MORE THAN
HALF OF IT ALREADY. I'M EVEN THINKING I MIGHT WRITE A
POEM ABOUT SKATEBOARDING TO GO AT THE FRONT. USUALLY I
HATE WRITING POETRY, BUT I LOVE SKATEBOARDING AND MS.
PACKER, MY OLD ENGLISH TEACHER, WAS ALWAYS SAYING WE
SHOULD WRITE STUFF ABOUT THINGS WE REALLY KNOW.

Sunday evening

WE HAD A BFC MEETING AT KAITLIN'S TODAY. I TOOK MY
PROJECT TO SEE WHAT THEY THOUGHT OF IT SO FAR—IF I DO
SAY SO MYSELF, I THINK IT'S TURNING OUT GREAT! AND THEY
TOTALLY AGREED! KAITLIN GAVE ME SOME HELP WITH THE
DESIGN OF MY FRONT COVER ON HER COMPUTER,
AND CALISTA HELPED ME WITH RESEARCH SO
I COULD ADD SOME STATISTICS, PIE CHARTS
AND MATH STUFF. I KEPT WORKING ON IT
ON THE COMPUTER AT HOME WHEN
I CAME BACK.

Monday after school

DEE-SASTER! DOUBLE DISASTER!
I WANTED TO TAKE MY PROJECT INTO
SCHOOL WITH ME BECAUSE NOELLE AND I
WERE GOING TO WORK ON IT IN THE LIBRARY
AFTER SCHOOL. I WENT TO GET ALL MY THINGS
FROM BY THE COMPUTER THIS MORNING AND HALF OF IT
WASN'T THERE!

MOM SAID SHE DIDN'T KNOW ANYTHING ABOUT IT AND MAYBE
DAD HAD IT BECAUSE HE WAS WORKING AT THE COMPUTER
BEFORE BREAKFAST. SHE CALLED DAD ON HIS CELL BUT HE SAID
HE DIDN'T KNOW ANYTHING ABOUT IT.

THEN HE CALLED MOM BACK AND SAID HE HAD BEEN
CLEANING UP THE DESK AND THERE WERE LOTS OF MAGAZINE
CLIPPINGS THAT HE THOUGHT WERE JUNK. SO HE THREW THEM
AWAY! HE'S THROWN AWAY HALF MY PROJECT! WORSE—THE
TRASH COLLECTORS CAME THIS MORNING! NOW MY PROJECT
IS IN A LANDFILL SITE SOMEWHERE!

ARGHHH! THIS PROJECT WAS MY BIG CHANCE TO IMPRESS
MY WAY BACK INTO MY OLD CLASS AND NOW IT'S FEEDING
SEAGULLS SOMEWHERE AND THERE'S NOTHING I CAN DO
ABOUT IT.

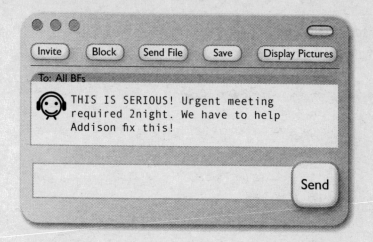

THIS IS SERIOUS! Urgent meeting required 2night. We have to help Addison fix this!

So we all got together. The girls have all sworn to help me redo the missing parts. I saw Elliot with Jake and told him. He's bringing over more mags to get more pics.

Am I going to be able to get out of this mess?

Tuesday after school

I worked all last night. Calista was really nice and helped me remember what was missing so that I could try to repeat it. Elliot brought the mags around this evening. He even helped me to cut out the pictures.

Some of them are even better than the ones I had before. He's just fantastic! Dad is really embarrassed.

HE SAID HE WOULD DO ANYTHING TO HELP. HUH! BUT THIS COULD
BE USEFUL FOR A FUTURE FAVOR!

WEDNESDAY—After school

OK, THINGS ARE LOOKING BETTER. ALL THIS WORK ON MY
PROJECT MUST HAVE WOKEN UP MY BRAIN. I GOT THE BEST
GRADE IN THE CLASS ON THE MATH TEST TODAY. MR. PALMER
WAS REALLY IMPRESSED.

THEN WE HAD A MEGA BFC MEETING. EVERYONE HELPED
ME COLLATE MY PROJECT. PHEW! IT WAS HARD WORK BUT YOU
KNOW WHAT? I THINK THIS NEW VERSION OF MY PROJECT JUST
MIGHT BE EVEN BETTER THAN THE ORIGINAL.

Thursday—After school

I CANNOT BELIEVE IT! I'M MOVING BACK TO MY OLD CLASSES
WITH MY BFS! YAY!!! NOELLE AND CALISTA TOLD MS. STREET
HOW HARD I'VE BEEN WORKING AND MS. FRASER TOLD HER
THAT MY MATH GRADE PLUS THE BRILLIANT WORK I DID
ON MY PROJECT PUT ME WAY BEYOND REMEDIAL CLASSES.

IT'S GONNA BE TOUGH, BUT I REALLY THINK I'M GONNA
KEEP UP WITH MY SCHOOLWORK AND STILL MANAGE TO ENJOY MY
SPORTS. I'M SO HAPPY. THANKS, ELLIOT, AND THANKS, BFC!

My Diary
by Kaitlin

friday after school

I can't believe it! I missed out on going to the mall with the BFC because Jen, my stepmom, wanted to get her hair done and guess who was the ONLY person she could think of to watch my baby brother Billy? ME, of course. I know I don't like malls that much but I love hanging with my BFs. Jen, apparently, doesn't KNOW that, so, while THEY were trying out new lip gloss, guess who was wiping baby goo off the sofa?

saturday 4:10 pm

When I told my big sister, Katie, she offered to take me to the mall instead.

"Come on, sis," she cooed into the phone in her ultra-trendy apartment, "it'll make up for you missing out yesterday. We could grab some lunch, go to the movies, maybe I'll even buy you a new top while we're there..."

So we went and, after Katie had picked out a cute printed tee for me from my fave store, "Wild Thing,"

118

we got in line for a smoothie from Super Smooth. Suddenly I heard someone chuckling behind me...someone who sounded suspiciously like Jake (I'd know his cute laugh anywhere). I turned around to say, "Hi!" but stopped in my tracks when I saw who he was with. Gianna Harris... Gasp! Were Jake and Gianna dating?

Maybe going to the mall isn't so great. In fact, here are three reasons why going to the mall seriously sucks:

1️⃣ You might see someone you know (total c-r-i-n-g-e if you're out with your dad).

2️⃣ You might see your crush with another girl!!!

3️⃣ The other girl might be **Gianna HARRIS!!!!!!!**

When Gianna developed a serious liking for my crush, Jake, I was devastated. She's the perfect match for Addison's older brother—pretty, popular, AND sporty. At first it seemed as if Jake liked her, too. But luckily for me the BFC came to the rescue with OPERATION Kaitlin. Aliesha gave me a master class in confidence, Addison tried to teach me some skateboarding skills and Noelle gave me some tips on flirting.

It didn't EXACTLY work out (I messed up BIG time) but it definitely brought me and Jake closer together—but not in a boyfriend-girlfriend way.

Meanwhile, Gianna started dating Dougie, a cute guy from our class that she'd liked for ages. So, things almost turned out perfectly...until now, that is.

So I did what any normal human being would do in a similar situation (i.e. spotting your crush out with another girl), I hid. I bent down to fiddle with my shoe, the floor, and the hem of my skirt, anything to prevent Jake and Gianna from seeing me.

"Are you okay, Kaitlin?" my sister asked, crouching down to join me on the floor. "What have you lost?"

"Oh, uh, nothing," I replied, slowly standing back up and looking around to see if Jake and Gianna were gone. They were. "I just thought I'd dropped something, that's all." I felt my bottom lip quiver. "Actually, I don't think I feel like a smoothie right now, Katie. Can you take me home, please?"

I couldn't face bumping into Gianna and Jake in the mall

again. Luckily, my sister took one look at my watery eyes, and gave in.

So here I am, back in my room, trying to stop crying. I'm probably being silly.

I mean, I once thought Dina the Diva herself was out on a date with Jake (when she used to like him) but really she was just finding a way to get at the BFC (l-o-n-g story). So maybe Gianna and Jake aren't dating. But then why were they out together???

I have to text Addison to see if she knows anything...

Message

Hey, is your bruv dBing
Gianna? Saw them at mall
2getha x

BACK   REPLY

So if Gianna and Jake really are dating this time, I'll just have to be all grown up about it and move on from my crush. As soon as I stop thinking about him, that is.

Wait, my phone's ringing...

saturday 4:30 pm

It was Addison. She doesn't know why Jake and Gianna were together at the mall but she doesn't think I have anything to worry about.

"I know what," she said down the phone. "Why don't you come over tonight and we can watch a DVD."

"How will that help?" I asked.

"We could watch that new action movie Jake's just been DYING to see," she giggled. "After all, it'll be easier to find out if he likes you if you're right here under his nose."

saturday 9 pm

Once again, Jen's ruined my life.

"Sorry Kaitlin," she said. "Me and your dad have got last minute movie tickets and we need a babysitter. I didn't think you'd mind. Can't you see Addison tomorrow?"

I might as well get used to it. Gianna's going to end up dating Jake if only because she's actually allowed to leave the house once in a millennium!

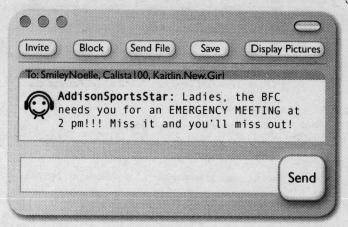

Invite | Block | Send File | Save | Display Pictures

To: SmileyNoelle, Calista100, Kaitlin.New.Girl

AddisonSportsStar: Ladies, the BFC needs you for an EMERGENCY MEETING at 2 pm!!! Miss it and you'll miss out!

Send

I'm not sure I can face going to a Best Friends' Club meeting. I hardly slept at all last night. I was so mad with Jen and I was worrying about the Gianna-Jake sitch. Still, maybe it will take my mind off things...

sunday 6 pm

I'm SO glad I went to the meeting. Aliesha had the most exciting news EVER!!! I'm just going to check my e-mail before dinner. Noelle promised to send us the minutes...

From:	Noelle Roberts < SmileyNoelle@bfc.com
To:	Kaitlin.New.Girl@bfc.com, AddisonSportsStar@bfc.com, Calista100@bfc.com, Aliesha4eva@bfc.com
Subject:	BFC minutes (i.e. what we talked about)

Verdana   10   **B** *I* <u>U</u>

<u>Time and Place of Meeting</u>: Sunday afternoon, Aliesha and Noelle's house, Aliesha's bedroom.

<u>Members Present</u>: Noelle, Kaitlin, Aliesha, Addison, Calista

<u>Discussion one:</u>   PAR-TAY

<u>Objective:</u>   The community youth center is putting on a party and EVERYONE is going!!!

<u>Action:</u>   Convince our parents that we HAVE to go, and discuss outfits at the next BFC meeting on Tuesday, at Calista's house.

<u>Discussion two:</u>   (never got around to this because we couldn't stop talking about the party and then it was time for everyone to go home!)

Yours sincerely,
Noelle
BFC Secretary

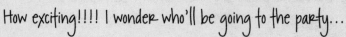

How exciting!!!! I wonder who'll be going to the party...

List of Possible Guests Going to the Party at the Youth Center

1.) The BFC (hopefully).

2.) Jake (please let him go, pleeeease).

3.) Gianna??? After all, she's friends with Calista these days, even though she'd not part of the BFC... and if Gianna AND Jake go, then they might kiss. I don't want to be around to see them cuddling in a corner somewhere. **EW!**

sunday 7:30 pm

OK. That's it! I'm NEVER talking to Jen again. Guess who can't go to the party because she's babysitting for her baby brother? AGAIN.

Dad and Jen have booked a table at some swanky restaurant, so my Saturday night will be spent watching Billy dribble in his sleep.

This time I actually screamed at Jen. "Why is YOUR social life so much more important than mine?"

Dad and Jen just stood there staring dumbly while

I stomped out of the room. It is soooo not fair!

Well, at least I won't have to watch Gianna and Jake drooling over each other...

But I suppose I'm going to have to HEAR about it...

Invite | **Block** | **Send File** | **Save** | **Display Pictures**

To: SmileyNoelle, Calista100, Aliesha4eva, AddisonSportsStar

Kaitlin.New.Girl: Guess who can't go to the party on Saturday! I've been roped into babysitting.

Aliesha4eva: No way! Seriously??? But you HAVE to go! You'll be missing the best party EVER!

SmileyNoelle: Yeah, this could be the perfect opportunity for you and Jake to finally get together...

Kaitlin.New.Girl: I've been crowned queen of babysitting. Watching Billy is now officially My Life.

Calista100: How are you ever going to get Jake to notice you?

Kaitlin.New.Girl: What's the point? Jake likes Gianna anyway. I saw them at the mall together. Anyway, who cares? I'm so over Jake...

Send

Okay, so that's not entirely true—it's actually not true at all. But I had to find a way to get the BFs off my back. I still can't believe that I'm not going to the party, but maybe it's for the best.

wednesday 5 pm

I felt so left out at the BFC meeting last night. Everyone was trying on clothes and giving each other makeovers in preparation for the party on Saturday.

"I feel bad about you not going, Kait," she said, when we were taking turns doing each other's nails. "Maybe we shouldn't go either and stay with you."

"Yeah," Aliesha added with a wink, "we could have a PJ party and try and lose Billy again."

Ha, ha! Not. I was seriously scared when that happened last time. Thankfully, Noelle found him before Dad and Jen ever found out.

"Thanks for the offer," I replied, "but you guys go ahead. There'll be other parties I can go to in the future." (So long as Jen doesn't want to go out, I thought.)

friday 4:10 pm

I don't think I can take much more of this. Everyone is so excited about tomorrow night's party. I'm just going to bury my head in my art project (I'm designing a stage set for the next school production) to take my mind off it.

saturday 7:30 pm

So, there I was, dressed in my most comfy PJs, eating strawberry cheesecake ice cream from the carton (Jen would freak if she knew that), watching a chick-flick, with Billy tucked up asleep in his crib.

Suddenly my cell rang. It was Jake.

"Hey, Kaitlin," he crooned into my ear, making my knees go weak. I could hear music pumping away in the background. "I was hoping to see you here at the party."

"Oh, hi, Jake," I replied, trying to sound cool and calm. "I'm babysitting Billy so I couldn't make it."

"That's a shame," he replied. "Well, uh, can I come

128

over and see you?"

"What about Gianna?" I burst out. So much for being cool and calm, but I had to know what was going on.

"Gianna? What about Gianna?" Jake repeated.

"I saw you. Together. At the mall." I said quietly.

"What?" Jake asked. "Oh, THAT. Addison mentioned you were at the mall—too bad I missed you. Me and Gianna just bumped into each other. We spoke for about a minute before going our separate ways."

"Oh," I replied. It slowly began to sink in. Jake and Gianna weren't together. I'd gotten my signals completely crossed. How embarrassing!!!! What an idiot...

"Kaitlin, are you still there?" asked Jake, interrupting my train of thought. "So, can I see you tonight?"

I looked down at my oh-so-comfy but oh-so-ugly PJs, with a bit of Billy dribble stain down the front.

"We-e-ell," I said slowly, "I'm kind of busy right now..." then added, "but I could see you tomorrow. If you're free, that is."

"Cool," Jake said, warmly. "Tomorrow would be great. Shall we meet at your house?"

"It's a date," I said, then cringed. What if it wasn't a date? What if we were just seeing each other as friends? What if...?"

"It's a date!!!" Jake confirmed.

So, that's it. Jake's coming over to my house. Tomorrow. And it's a date!!!

saturday 10 pm

Guess what? Jen and Dad had a talk while they were out. They admitted they'd been using my babysitting services too much. They said that in the future they'll find someone else to watch Billy if our dates clash. So of course I told them I'd get Gianna's number. After all, she wants the work. And it'll give her something to do while I'm seeing Jake! I can't wait to tell the BFC... I wonder if they're back from the party yet?

Saturday 8:30 am

Noelle is totally overexcited. Twice already this morning she's run into my room and jumped up and down on my bed. And all because Ben's visiting for the weekend. Don't get me wrong. I'm happy for her, but when said jumping up and down happens:

a) At 6:17 am AND 6:50 am,

b) when I'm still asleep in the bed she's jumping up and down on, it's seriously hard to join in her excitement!

Ooh, hang on, it's a text message from Kaitlin:

BFCAHO stands for Best Friends' Club And Hangers On.

Not exactly catchy is it?

MEET @ MY HOUSE @ 9.30 SHARP 4 1ST BFCAHO OUTING 2 PLANET FUN THEME PARK!!! XOX

BACK   REPLY

Kaitlin came up with it. Let's just say she's much better with design than she is with words!! With the rest of the BFCs totally love-

132

struck, I'm seriously starting to feel like one of the hangers on.

Saturday 9 pm

Well, the day started pretty much as I expected. Talk about Couple Central. When we met at Kaitlin's house, Calista and Zac and Addison and Elliot spent the whole time talking about the movie they'd seen on a double-date last night. As for Ben and Noelle, you'd think they'd been separated for a year, not a few weeks.

Kaitlin's mom and Addison's mom were driving us to the theme park in two cars, so as soon as they unlocked the car doors, all the couples scrambled in to sit next to each other. I got stuck in a car with Kaitlin and Jake, who spent the whole time giggling together and staring into each other's eyes—totally barf-making behavior.

It didn't get much better once we got to Planet Fun. I was still annoyed from the journey and refused to talk to anyone. I sulked as the others agreed to split up and meet back at the

Information Point a while later. What happened to our unwritten rule:

Best Friends Are Forever, Boys Are Whatever?

That's what I want to know.

"Why don't you hang around with me and Ben, Aliesha?" asked Noelle.

"What, and get in the way of love's young dream?" I said sarcastically, scuffing the toe of my left sneaker on the sidewalk.

"Don't be silly," smiled Noelle, linking her arm through mine. "It'll be fun, won't it, Ben?"

I grinned at her. "OK, I get to pick the first ride!"

Noelle rolled her eyes. "As long as it's not the biggest, fastest, scariest roller-coaster. You know I can't stand them."

I glared at my twin. That was exactly what I wanted to go on.

"I suppose you'd rather go on the teacups," I said scathingly.

Noelle reddened. "Well, yes, I would, actually," she said.

"Noelle!" I wailed. "They're for babies!"

"They're not," she said.

"They are!"

"They're not."

"Are too."

"Are not."

"Are."

"Aren't."

"Are."

"Aren't."

"Oh shut up."

"You shut up."

"You."

"No, you."

"No, you."

At this point, Ben interrupted.

"Uh, much as I hate to end this conversation," he said, "I agree with Noelle."

"What a surprise!" I muttered.

Noelle glowered at me.

"Well, he is your boyfriend," I said. "Obviously he's going to agree with you."

"No, he isn't," Noelle retorted.

"Yes, he is."

"No. He. Isn't."

135

"Yes. He. Is."

"No, he i . . ."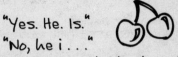

"Please don't start all that again,"
pleaded Ben. He looked at me. "It's not just
because she's my girlfriend."

"Yeah, right!" I muttered.

"It's not!" said Ben. "It's actually cos I'm
scared of heights."

I stared at him in disbelief.

"You two really are the perfect match,"
I grumbled.

"Well, enjoy your kiddie rides. I'm going to have
some real fun."

And without a backward glance I stomped off.
Well, I wasn't wasting my time on the wussy rides.
Not me. No way. I'd spend the day riding the
scariest rides the park had to offer. And what's
more, I was going to have an awesome time.

A few rides later, I headed for the Loop
Torpedo—the biggest, most famous ride at the
park. There were a lot of people already waiting. I
sighed loudly and walked toward the end of the
line. I totally perked up, though, when I saw what—
or more precisely who—would be standing in front

136

of me. A total vision of gorgeousness—tall and thin, with dark floppy hair and striking blue eyes—was leaning against the rail. I grinned to myself and hurried toward the end of the line.

Things were definitely starting to look up.

Suddenly someone bumped into me from behind and I went flying past the Vision of Gorge.

"Hey!" he shouted. "There's a line!"

"I know!" I said.

"So why are you barging in, then?" he asked.

"I wasn't," I glared at him. "Someone shoved me."

"A likely story," he said. "You're the fifth person who's tried to jump the line since I've been here. What makes you think you're so special?"

"I don't! I wasn't!" I practically shouted. Even through my anger, I couldn't help noticing that he looked more than a smidgen like Mickey Dean—lead singer of the Beat Boyz and my ideal man.

"And you obviously think you're perfect," I said.

"If the shoe fits . . ." he winked.

I stared at him, not knowing whether to laugh or explode with rage. Just then a man standing behind me tapped me on the shoulder.

"Could you and your boyfriend hurry up, please? You're holding up the line."

"He's not my boyfriend," I said.

"Yeah, you wish," said the boy, grinning at me. Then he clambered onto the last space on the ride. I watched irritatedly as he pulled the safety harness over himself. As the roller-coaster pulled away, he waved to me.

Ten minutes later, still on a high from the Loop Tornado, I excitedly made my way toward the Defier—one of those rides that lifts you up in the air just to let you drop. I hurried toward the line. I stopped in my tracks as I saw the Mickey Dean-a-like a few people ahead of me. Quickly I ducked behind the woman in front of me, who fortunately was carrying a backpack almost as big as herself.

I let out a sigh of relief. Cautiously, I peeked out from behind the backpack. Luckily he wasn't looking in my direction. I couldn't help noticing that he was wearing a T-shirt that was almost identical to the one Mickey Dean had worn in his video. What was I doing? Honestly, I was acting like I liked him.

As if I could like anyone so arrogant. Even if he

did have gorgeous blue eyes. I jumped as someone poked me in the shoulder.

"Well, well, well," said a familiar-sounding drawl. "We must stop meeting like this."

The Mickey Dean-a-like was standing in front of me. I glared at him.

"Are you following me?" he asked.

"As if!" I snorted..

"Oh, come on!" said the boy.

"Don't flatter yourself," I snorted. "I just happen to like scary rides. When I saw you in the line again, I tried to hide because I didn't want to talk to you. OK?"

"Really?" he said, looking amused.

"Yes!" I snapped. "What, you think girls are crawling all over themselves to chat with you?" (Inside, I knew I was SO crawling all over myself to talk with him but, whatever, I wasn't going to admit that!)

"So you like scary rides, huh?" he asked. "I'm surprised."

"Really? What do you mean by that?" I asked.

"Well," he said, "girls who look like you usually don't."

"What do you mean?" I asked testily.

"Well, you know, girls who look girly."

I glared at him. "What?"

"I meant it as a compliment," he said. "Most girls are too busy worrying about their hair or their lip gloss to enjoy roller-coasters."

I felt myself flush redder than my sweatshirt. What was going on? Aliesha does NOT blush. Especially in front of boys. Uh-uh. Not me. No way.

"Well, I'm not like that," I said.

"I can tell," he grinned and held out his hand. "Luke Connor."

"Aliesha Roberts," I said, grasping his hand and hoping my hands weren't as sweaty as they felt.

"It's a pleasure to meet you, Aliesha," he said. 'Now, without wanting to sound cheesy, what's a nice girl like you doing all alone in a place like this?"

Suddenly I glanced at my watch. Nooooo! I was over half an hour late to meet everyone at the Information Point. But why hadn't they texted me? I pulled my phone out of my pocket. It was dead. I'd forgotten to charge it that morning.

"I've got to go!" I wailed. "I'm late to meet my friends. My phone's dead. So they have no way of contacting me. They're going to be really worried."

I stared around me in panic. "Which way's the Information Point?"

"This way," Luke said, grabbing my hand and pulling me through the crowd. I blushed with pleasure. He. Was. Holding. My. Hand. Fortunately, it was mega-warm in the sunshine. My red cheeks could easily have been caused by overheating, not necessarily by me going all weak-kneed.

Five minutes later, we skidded to a halt by the Information Point. There was no sign of the others. I blinked back tears. I know I'd acted like a spoiled brat earlier, but they wouldn't go without me. Would they?

"I . . . I . . . think they've left," I said, turning away from Luke so he wouldn't see the tears that were threatening to spill.

Luke spun me around and grinned at me.

"It's not funny," I practically shouted at him.

Luke started to speak, but I wasn't finished.

"My friends have gone home without me. And all you can do is stand there laughing."

Luke shook his head. "Do you ever shut up?" he asked. I gaped at him. Luke winked at me.

"That's better," he said. "Now, look over there." I looked where he was pointing and saw a jeep with Planet Fun written all over it, heading toward me. A jeep that was full of people waving at me. People who looked a lot like Noelle, Calista, Kaitlin, Addison, Ben, Elliot, Jake, and Zac. As the jeep shuddered to a halt, Noelle flung herself out of it and ran toward me.

"Where have you been?" she asked, throwing her arms around me. "I've been so worried. We've searched the whole park for you."

"I thought you left without me!" I said.

Noelle stepped back and looked at me. "Aliesha, you're my twin sister. I'd never leave without you."

"And neither would we," said Calista, walking up behind us with Addison and Kaitlin and joining in the hug.

"Hey, is this a private hug or can anyone join in?"

asked Ben. Soon I was caught up in a BFCAHO group hug.

I suddenly noticed Luke standing next to us, looking awkward. I broke away from the group and grinned at him. "Guys, this is Luke."

"Hi!" everyone chorused. Calista grinned at me. "Cute!" she mouthed.

"Um, I've got to go," said Luke.

My heart plummeted. "OK," I said. "Uh, thanks for all your help."

"No problem," said Luke. "If you give me your cell number maybe we could go on some more scary rides together sometime."

As I watched him walk away a few minutes later, I couldn't help but think that maybe I'd found my very own Hanger On. And that maybe a few more BFCAHO outings wouldn't be such a bad idea after all.

BFC ink.
best friends Club, ink
Stick Together. Friends Forever!
Hang out with your BFFs!
Be yourself!
SHARE SECRETS
Look for
Best Friends Club, Ink.
Dolls, Toys and Accessories
for even More BFF Fun!